CW00498819

CONTACT!

A MILITARY HORROR ANTHOLOGY

EDITED BY

CHRIS MCINALLY

COPYRIGHT © SCREAMING BANSHEE PRESS, 2021

Cover art by Matt James

'SOFTBAIT' © DAN RABARTS, 2021

'THE SHATTERING' © DANIELE BONFANTI, 2021

'LABYRINTH' © WILLIAM MEIKLE, 2021

'BONESAW RIDGE' © LUCAS PEDERSON, 2021

'A MAN OF HIS WORD' © ALISTER HODGE, 2021

'BLACK ICE' © R.F. BLACKSTONE, 2021

'INTO THE GEYSERLAND' © LEE MURRAY, 2021

'THE BUBBLE BURSTS' © DUSTIN DREYLING, 2021

'THE APOCALYPSE DRIVE' © JUSTIN COATES, 2021

SOFTBAIT

Dan Rabarts

For a second Whero was back on the farm, spotlighting rabbits, lights raking the bush. The growl of the engine and the hiss of tyres in mud reminded him of home, the difference being that he was staring down a machinegun barrel instead of a rifle. It used to be his dad's old ute, with the spotlights on the roof-rack and his .22 gripped easily in both hands. But for all that the scale of the operation had changed, running down militia in the jungle of East Timor was fundamentally much the same as spotlighting.

Speeding through the dark, torchlight cutting sharp shadows through the vegetation, straining to spot something he could take a shot at. Little bastards, rabbits. Eating everything, digging holes, shitting everywhere. Spreading diseases to the sheep and cows, cutting into the *whanau's* profits. Hard enough to make a living farming the dry reaches of New Zealand's East Cape on a small family plot without the little bastards making life even more difficult. They made for good eating if there was anything left of them by the time the .22 round had done its work, but mostly they were a pest. Spotlighting was a necessary part of being a farmer's son, and Whero enjoyed the thrill of it more than the spoils, anyway. There was a rush that came when the dark grass suddenly burst to life with long, lean limbs, little buggers darting for safety, the animals' fear balanced against the cold weight of the rifle, the calm cool of the trigger, that moment when he held life in his fingers and delivered that bright sharp cough of death, splintering the night. Whero had always got a thrill from seeing them run, watching them arc head over feet as a bullet took them in the rump or the shoulder or the head, leaving them in contorted twitching heaps on the grass. It wasn't the killing he enjoyed. It was doing something he knew needed doing. Some things just had to be done.

East Timor was much the same as the farm; just bigger rabbits. Lance Corporal Whero Maeke *would* think of them as men if they didn't act like animals that needed to be put down for the things they did. Shit made him angry, and angry wasn't good when you're on the end of a MAG 58. So, he thought of them as animals, *pests*, and that made it easier. Made him calm again. Just doing shit that needed to be done, clearing out the vermin. Whero didn't give two cold craps whose religion had been here first, or which tribe thought they had a right to slaughter the other for their land and their pigs, or whatever the hell reason the New Zealand Army was here along with the rest of the INTERFET force, jamming their noses into another country's business. Terms like 'Independence' and 'Freedom Fighting' and 'Peacekeeping' don't mean much when you're the one some bastard in a muddy Land Rover is shooting at, and someone else is tossing home-made explosives into the bar where you're trying to enjoy a quiet beer to rinse away the day's sweat.

There'd been a festival going on, some backwater fertility thing, the village folk prancing through the streets of Tutuala, banging drums and waving painted masks in front of their faces, before the shit hit the fan. Falloon was going on about what the parade meant, walking encyclopaedia that he was. Soothing the forest spirits or something. *Taniwha*, Whero had thought. Or *kehua*. Monsters and ghosts.

One minute they'd been drinking as the evening dusk chilled towards night, the next, they were caught up in a firefight. Here, like at home, he had his orders, and those orders were to shoot the rabbits. Thinking about it that way made it all much clearer. Less blurred by *conscience*. The rush of wind as the Unimog bounced along the jungle path cooled his skin, and he hoped it would last. Not much aircon back at base. In East Timor, he sweated twenty-four/seven beneath his flak jacket and helmet.

"Anyone got visual?" Melinda 'Barky' Barker said, her voice coming through Whero's earpiece in a hiss of static.

Barky was braced in the back of the Unimog, swinging the xenon spotlight across the jungle in slow, deliberate arcs. Scanning for anywhere the militia's Land Rover could've slipped off the main road, if that's what you'd call this potholed, unsealed track through the rainforest.

Whero just shook his head and watched the trees through his night-vision goggles, careful not to look directly into the bright xenon beam as it punched through the undergrowth. More voices rattled along the comms; Lassey driving, Corporal Ramen up there with him, the two new guys down the back with their Steyrs at their shoulders, wet behind the ears. Hadn't been on task long enough to earn themselves nicknames yet. Probably signed up thinking they'd never actually get shot at. *Welcome to East Timor, boys.* Whero tuned out the chatter to concentrate on the dark.

"There!" Whero shouted, as something big lurched through his periphery beyond the treeline. In a flurry, both torch and machinegun spun. Whero hunted for the target, whatever he'd seen out the corner of his eye, big enough to be a Land Rover, for sure, but where was it?

A Steyr cracked.

"Who's firing?" Ramen yelled from the cab.

"Me, Corporal. It's Jordan," the greenie warbled down the line, his voice shaky. Jitters, and a rifle in hand. Not a good combination.

"Shooting at what, Private?"

Jordan shrugged. "Not sure, Corp. Thought I saw something."

"Confirm your targets before you fire, lads. You know this shit."

"Yessir."

Whero said nothing, glad it wasn't him getting reamed by the Corporal, because he'd only been a heartbeat away from pulling the trigger himself. Maybe it was the training, or all those nights out shooting rabbits, but he needed something in his sights before he'd shoot. And there *had been* something—in fact, he was sure there *was* something—but until he could see it, he'd hold his fire. One shot from a rifle into the jungle? That's an ear-bashing from the Corp. Opening up with reckless abandon with a MAG 58 without confirming the presence of an enemy target? That's getting written up, getting sent home on the next Hercules out. Going back to civilian life, or worse if it turned out there was a quiet sleeping village behind those layers of shadowed vegetation the MAG was staring down. Whero didn't want to make himself an international incident. But what'd he seen?

Never mind.

The Unimog slowed as they reached a branch in the jungle track. "Barky, swing that torch over here," Ramen ordered.

Whero continued to scan the trees as Barky and the Corporal checked out the tracks in the mud. He tried not to think too hard about how they'd ended up out here, miles from town, without any backup or support. Almost like the attack hadn't been meant to hurt anyone but only to...lure them away?

Falloon and Jordan were talking, their mouthpieces folded down. "This is all that's left of Timor's old rainforests," Falloon said. "Europeans came in the sixteenth century and harvested the sandalwood forest, and most of the rest of the island's been cleared for cash crops like cocoa and coffee."

"So why's it so fucking hard to find a decent latte around here?" Jordan joked, his voice just this side of slipping into childlike terror.

"Older than civilisation, this stretch of jungle," Falloon went on, unperturbed. "Most of the island's Catholic, but they still practice the old faiths out here. Traditional gods, spirits, all that. The Indonesians tried to eliminate the pagan religions by outlawing them, after the Portuguese pulled out in the seventies, but there are still pockets."

"You read this shit in *Lonely Planet*?" Jordan mocked.

Falloon shrugged. "Pays to know the enemy, right?"

4

Whero grinned, bleak in the darkness. *All just rabbits.* "Not meant to think of them as the enemy, bro," he said. "That's not the policy. We're *peacekeepers.*" Engagement policy was very clear. The INTERFET wasn't here to start a war, but to prevent one. They weren't invaders, but defenders. That was the official line. The Unimog jerked back into motion and they turned left, following a narrower track deeper into the primeval jungle. Whero shot a look at Barky. "Fresh tracks?" he said.

"Looks like it." Barky swung the torch around, lighting up the track. A pair of treads led through the mud, disappearing under the accelerating Unimog. Whero's gaze lingered on the tracks a moment longer before peripheral movement snapped his eyes back to the jungle and the darkness beyond. Shapes on the path, a glimpse of something in the mud, in the light of the xenon, all vanishing shadow and sinking mud. Had that been...animal prints?

Whero whipped his head around to stare into the black behind the Unimog. Swear to god that'd looked like rabbit prints, only too big to be rabbit prints. Fucking huge. Whero shook his head, sniffed. Trick of the light. Nothing that big on this island. Nowhere for it to hide.

...all that's left of Timor's old rainforests...

Whero suppressed the shudder that rippled down his spine and focused on the road. The jungle closed in tighter around them. He spat over the side, hating that he was letting his nerves get to him. Nothing out here but rats and monkeys and birds.

The Unimog slewed to a stop. An engine grumbled in the bush ahead.

"Barky," Ramen called.

Barker swung the torch around to light up the rear section of a Land Rover, the same one that'd hurtled out of the bush and skidded up alongside the bar in Tutuala, the militia in the back firing randomly and lobbing flaming bottles at the NZDF soldiers. At the time, Whero hadn't thought it strange they were shooting into the air and not at them, nor into the crowd; he'd been too busy diving

5

for cover, grabbing his rifle, scrambling to return fire. Through the molotovs scouring flames he'd seen the militiamen, their eyes wide and white like possums in headlights, before the Land Rover had revved and sped away in a spray of mud. The kiwis had fired back, but in the confusion and panic they hadn't been able to get off a clear shot. The Unimog was parked close by, untouched by enemy fire, and they were trained for this, weren't they?

But now, staring at the abandoned wagon idling on the side of the track, Whero's blood chilled. The militia had had them, dead to rights, back in the village. Some of the fireteam should've been dead or wounded after a flash attack like that. But the militia had been firing randomly, not a single round coming close to the soldiers—or the civilians, for that matter. A moment of chaos and violence, and the kiwis had rushed to pursue the offenders. This was the mission; this was why they were on this muddy scrap of an island. Now here they were, miles from town, miles from *anywhere*, the last light long since drained from the sky, and the militia had melted away into the jungle, on foot. The hairs on Whero's neck stood up. Chasing down a target as big as a Land Rover was one thing, but the militia had ditched the vehicle. Pursuing armed men in their own territory, in the dark, without backup or fire support? That was something else altogether. *Fuck* that.

"What's that smell?" Jordan said from the back. Whero didn't like the way the newbie's Steyr trembled in his grip. Jordan was shit-scared. Not a good thing. Whero sniffed.

"Smells like gas," Barky said. "What the...?"

The flames came from both directions at once, twin lances of bright heat rushing out of the wet rainforest to surround the Unimog and the Land Rover.

"Get down!"

Whero's yell came too late for Falloon, as the petrol-soaked earth blazed up around them. The greenie stumbled back, clutching his face, his rifle discharging with a boom as he fell, screeching like a stuck pig. Someone else yelped in pain, presumably Jordan, but Whero didn't see who as he and Barky dropped to the Unimog's deck. Then the truck was moving, reversing at speed through the flames and spinning hard. Something heavy fell in the mud beside the Unimog. Whero braced himself against the back of the cab and hauled himself upright on the machinegun bracket, fighting the hurtling Unimog's momentum and the wash of heat from the flames. There was shouting in his ear, but the words were lost in the roar of the fire.

Only seconds before...

The Land Rover erupted. The concussion wave drove outwards before the wall of flame and shrapnel that boiled from the vehicle, probably loaded with several kilos of plastic explosive. Whero ducked as the fireball swept over them, the Unimog lifting and sliding, the right-hand tyres losing their grip and sliding into a sodden gully beside the track. Whero's feet went out from under him but he clung doggedly to the MAG 58's grips, the gun tilting wildly into the sky as his weight snapped it upwards. Barky skidded down the suddenly pitching flatbed on her knees, the torch's gimbal disconnecting with a metallic snap, power cable whipping out of its socket. The truck collided with something solid, a tree or a rock, and stopped its slide. Barky and Falloon both slammed into the truck's side with a bone-jarring crunch.

Then there were gunshots, and the hot ring of bullets ricocheting off the Unimog's chassis, glass splintering. Not firing randomly this time, were they? *Fuckers.*

Whero tuned out the voices in his earpiece—Falloon, whimpering, muttering something about how he couldn't see, *can't see*; Jordan, somewhere, screaming; Barky, calling down the comms for the medic; Ramen, shouting orders that no-one could follow because all hell was breaking loose and it was all they could do to stay on their feet—and tried to get his bearings. For the moment, he was concealed from the bush by the side of the truck, but that wouldn't be the case for long. If he were a militiaman, he'd have an RPG ready to fire right now, targeting the truck's belly. If they hadn't anticipated the truck would go into the slough, he might have time. Still, he didn't want to poke his head out for a look. They'd probably be circling around to get a clear shot.

Bracing his legs against the side of the truck, he angled the MAG 58 towards the bush, confirmed Jordan wasn't in his line of fire, and gripped the trigger. The hammer of the machinegun lit up the night, shredding the jungle, shuddering through his shoulders. Whero panned the gun, spraying bright rounds in a wide arc. Confirmed targets be damned when people were blowing up booby-trapped Land Rovers and taking pot shots at you from the treeline.

He stopped firing. Over the ringing in his ears, the metallic clatter of hot shell casings rolling down the flatdeck, and the crackle of flames, a strange quiet descended. No more gunshots from the bush. Even Falloon had shut up. But Jordan was out there somewhere, shouting. Screaming?

"Maeke? Barky?"

"Corp."

"Corp."

"Sitrep?"

"Falloon's down, suspect minor burns," Barky reported, clambering across to where Falloon lay huddled in a foetal ball in the corner. "He'll be OK with a bit of TLC. Not sure about Jordan. He's not back here."

Whero snuck a peek around the side of the cab. Beyond the flames, there was only the darkness of the jungle. The fire made his night-vision goggles useless, so he tugged them down. Somehow, the firelit bush was worse.

"We need to secure the site. Monitor the treeline. I'm sending Hwang."

"Copy," Barky said.

The cab door opened and Hwang appeared, the medic throwing his pack ahead of him as he hauled himself into the truck's sloping rear. Lassey revved the engine, the wheels gripping mud, gaining traction, slipping, sliding. They were meant to be so good, these trucks, but were they really? Whero dimly remembered some statistic about how since Vietnam more NZDF soldiers had died in Unimog accidents than in the line of fire. Not exactly optimal. He nodded at Hwang and turned his attention back to the clearing, the muddy road, focusing on relaxing his breathing, listening for sounds of movement in the bush. But all he could hear was Jordan out there, shouting up a storm. Where the hell was he? Had he been thrown past the wall of flame by the explosion? Onto the road, or into the bush? Whero couldn't see him, so he must be in the bush. And why wasn't he shutting the hell up? Why give away his position? So green.

Then the shouts turned to screams, thick with terror, even over the crackling of the burning bush, the rev of the Unimog's engine, the squelch of flying mud, the thunder of blood rushing in Whero's ears, and Falloon's whimpers of pain.

Then the body came flying from the trees. It flopped through the air like a broken rag doll, limbs flailing as it twisted and landed with a sickening crunch on the road. Jungle fatigues, drenched in blood. Unmoving.

"Jordan!" Whero moved to go to the injured—*dead?*—solider.

"Stay there, Maeke!" Ramen shouted and leapt from the cab.

"Corp!" The fear rose like an urge to vomit. But Whero gripped his weapon hard, ready to unleash hell on the jungle and whoever—*whatever*—was out there, the moment they showed themselves. Jordan hadn't walked back onto the road and collapsed. He'd been *thrown*, tossed like a toy. Blood pooled around him in a muddy arc that flickered in the dying firelight. Whero had seen blood like that before, and he doubted anything short of a chopper evac was going to be enough to save the young fullah, if he wasn't dead already. A dark spill around the body suggested entrails flung wide.

They weren't facing militiamen anymore. There were no more gunshots, and any paramilitary force worth their salt would've

9

taken advantage of the Kiwis being flatfooted by now and finished them. No, they were gone. Whero got the awful sense that this was nothing to do with the politics of East Timor and her bully-boy neighbour; they'd been led here, trapped, lured into the territory of whatever it was out there in the trees. Whatever was *hunting them.* Whero didn't want to be a rabbit.

Something moved, half-formed, twisting and leaping through the dark.

"Corp!" Whero shouted, catching movement out of the corner of his eye.

He spun, the MAG 58 swivelling, heavy, limp, not fast enough. Even as he pulled the trigger and the jungle lit up, he knew he'd missed. The shape, too fast to see, burst from the trees, all impossibly long limbs and teeth white as the moon, and then was gone again, a shadow strobing in the light of the machinegun's muzzle flash.

Corporal Ramen was no longer there either. His cries came back from the dark, growing distant. Full of pain and terror.

Then nothing.

Whero sucked down choking breaths. *What the hell?* "Man down! Repeat, man down! Lassey, you see that?"

"The fuck were you shooting at, bro?" Lassey shouted back. He hadn't seen…hadn't seen those limbs, the bright sharp glint of teeth. The ridiculously long ears, snapping against the flare of the muzzle flash like dark wings.

"Barky!" Whero spun, releasing the MAG 58 and grabbing his assault rifle from where it was racked. "Bring the torch."

"The hell, man?" Barky fixed him with a look that told him enough. Barky had seen it too. What it was, they didn't know. But she'd seen something.

"We sit here, we get picked off one by one. Hwang, stay low. Lassey, try to get us out of here. Barky, we need to get clear and gain some tactical ground."

Barky wavered for a moment, chewing her lip, the fear stretched tight across her forehead. Then she nodded. "Ramen's gone. That puts you in charge, I suppose."

"It does." Hefting their Steyrs, Whero and Barky slid over the side of the Unimog onto the lip of the slurry, hunkering into the shadow. "You ever go spotlighting as a kid?" Whero asked.

"Nuh-uh." Barky shook her head, flicking the torch off, its power cable dangling. Hopefully the battery would last. "But I know what you mean."

"Good." Whero signalled towards the trees behind them, where the line of burning petrol had originated. "Let's go."

Barky followed, slinging her rifle on her shoulder and drawing her Sig 9mm. "What are we looking for?" she hissed.

The line of scorched vegetation was easy enough to track. Hopefully it would lead them to the last place the militiamen had been, and they could pick up their trail through the bush. Whatever was picking off the fire squad like flies, the locals knew how to stay out of its reach.

"You remember that festival in the village, the masks that Falloon was going on about?"

"What about it?"

"It was some sort of ritual, Falloon kept yapping about fertility rites, I reckon he's just got it on the brain. But hear me out. You ever go pig hunting?"

"The hell does pig hunting have to do with the mask festival?"

"I reckon it's no coincidence that festival was on right at the same time we rocked up to the village. Like we've been baited, same way you bait a pig in the bush. Keep your eye out for movement. You see anything, you light it up with the torch, OK?"

"You mean anyone?"

"Anyone and *anything*."

Footprints in the mud, spent shell casings. Whero motioned for silence, bent double, and stalked through the rainforest in the direction the clutch of tracks led. Spread wide, deep. Running.

Softbait, is what they were. That's what his dad liked to call it, anyway. It was a technique his old man had adapted from a book he'd read, about homesteaders in North America drawing out wolves that were harrying stock. Hang a hunk of fresh meat, preferably lamb, on a hook in an open field, then lay low with a loaded gun. Soon enough, out comes the wolf, and *boom*. Bob's your uncle. Wolf pelts for the winter. Whero's dad had done the same thing to lure pigs in the bush, only he'd used sacks of overripe fruit and vegetables. Same principle, still drew in the pigs. It beat the hell out of walking through the bush for hours looking for hoofprints and pig shit. The soldiers were the softbait now, only this was a different hunt. What had Falloon been saying, back at that bar, with the villagers in their freaky masks and ridiculous get-up all leaping and prancing to the beat of those skin-tight drums and screeching flutes and waving torches? How the fertility rituals of these far-flung parts of Indonesia were bound up with sacrifice to the forest spirits? It all fit together.

Over the grumble of the Unimog came a ponderous low thumping of air, the distinct beat of rotors. Ramen must've radioed for backup before the shit hit the fan, or maybe Hwang had called in an evac. It'd be an Aussie Sea Hawk, despatched from a frigate on the Timor Sea. Only a few minutes away. "Chopper inbound."

"That's good. Falloon's hurt pretty bad."

"That's not what you told Ramen."

"Didn't need him screaming any louder, did we?"

Whero pulled up short. Electric lines snaked out of the bush and around a tree trunk, just along the edge of the road. Even without the torch the white putty of several kilos of plastic explosive were visible taped to the bark. He gestured. "This was their original plan," he whispered. "If we hadn't got stuck in that slurry, they would've blown the tree across the road, trapping us. Betcha it's the same on the other side."

"Where do the wires lead?" Barky breathed.

They turned, following the coils of cable. Whero dropped his NVGs back into position and scanned the jungle floor, his world turning green. He pointed.

Barky froze. They were both seeing the same thing, then. That was good. Meant he wasn't going completely fucking mental. The footprints had to be a foot long, narrow, padded, with the sharp imprint of claws at one end. Blood spattered the leaves and broken branches around them. The thing had come this way, with Jordan maybe, or Ramen.

"The fuck...?" Barky breathed.

"*Taniwha*," Whero replied, his voice barely above a hiss. He continued tracing the wires, Barky falling in behind him. "I know what I saw. It's our blood being spilled to appease the hunger of a forest spirit, that's why the militia didn't take us out when they had the chance. They didn't bring us here to kill us, but to feed the monster, so maybe it'll go back to sleep for another hundred years or some shit. When that chopper arrives, the monster's going to vanish and take Ramen with it. We've got about two minutes to draw it out and kill the fucking thing, or we lose more than just the Corporal, we lose his body too."

"You got a plan?"

Whero's jaw tightened, thinking fast. "We do what they were gonna do." He rounded a tree trunk to find the makeshift detonator, complete with battery pack and red plunger button, sitting in a plastic bag in the soggy bole of a tree fern. "Right," he said, and pointed through the trees towards the road. "I'm going down there. You've got the torch. When I get to the road, light up the truck."

Barky stiffened. "And?"

"When the fucker shows, I'll take a shot at it, draw it to me. When it moves, you hit that button."

"Lance-Corporal, that's fucking insane. You'll be blown to pieces."

"I won't be that close."

Whero jogged through the bush, passing the explosives-laden tree and jumping the slurry beside the road. Running several dozen meters down the track away from the Unimog, he turned and dropped to a crouch, lining up the truck in his scope. The bright lance of the xenon cut through the trees and outlined the back end of the truck, Falloon and Hwang. His softbait. The lambs laid out for the wolf, and he the huntsman lying in wait.

Then someone screamed, Ramen's body landing on the roof of the cab, and it was there, the creature a grotesquery lit up in the harsh ray from Barky's torch. It paused, a sinuous thing of elongated limbs and a narrow maw that flickered with long, impossibly sharp teeth. Blood drenched its white fur. Biggest fucking rabbit Whero had ever seen, and he shuddered. The beast stopped for a heartbeat, as if deciding whether to scoop up another victim from the back of the truck, or to leap for the unexpected light source in the bush.

Whero fired. One shot, to gauge the line of fire, then two more, the Steyr barking in the night. The creature recoiled, twisted, vanished. There one second, gone the next, like a shadow fleeing an opening curtain.

The jungle erupted. Trees crashed down.

Lifted by the concussion, Whero flew backwards and landed hard on his back somewhere down the track. The wind exploded from his lungs in a hot burst, and for long gagging seconds he sucked on nothing, head ringing, exposed skin burning with heat and hot vapour.

More voices in his ear, garbled static, but he couldn't speak, couldn't breathe. Red haze, painting the night in blood. His limbs refused to move. He'd lost his rifle. For those few seconds he was helpless, a turtle overturned and kicking for purchase.

The shape loomed over him, a wavering, tottering tower of nightmare, white fur drenched in dappled red and black. Ash and blood, but not blood like he knew it. The creature wove, dipped, and Whero scrambled frantically for the knife at his belt. He'd seen many a rabbit clipped by a bullet, injured but not killed, so he knew by the way this creature swayed over him that it was wounded. Felt its regard, hurt and curious at this being beneath it, this prey, this *sacrifice*, that had damaged it so. He wasn't already dead because the monster was trying to decide what he was. Prey, or equal?

He was a rabbit hunter, motherfucker. And he was a soldier.

He thrust the knife upwards, jerking his arm into a straight line, finding flesh, tough and wiry. Wet heat spilled over his hand, thick and fetid, scoured him like hot mud. The monster howled, drew back in a lightning motion to strike.

Thunder buffeted the treetops, blazing light raking the road.

An assault rifle cracked from the bushes, tracer cutting the air over Whero's head.

Like not so much as a breath of wind disappearing through the bush, the thing was gone. More voices in his ear, the swarm of the Sea Hawk's searchlight illuminating the devastation on the road. Australian accents, tuning in to their frequency. The cavalry had arrived.

Barky appeared, dropping to a crouch in the mud beside him, her Steyr butted to her shoulder, sweeping back and forth. "What the fuck was it?"

Whero sagged into the mud, took in a slow painful breath. Ignored the radio chatter. Thought about rabbits, and pigs, and dying wolves, and how it hadn't been an animal looking down at him in that awful, endless moment, but something much worse. Something more ancient and terrifying, more hungry. Something vengeful, which now had a taste for him.

He was the animal. And the hunter never abandons the hunt.

The Sea Hawk descended, its spotlight blinding. The jungle rippled under its down-draught, all fire and shadow.

"Rabbits," Whero Maeke said, laughing at the black sky above, eyes wide and shining. "We're all just rabbits."

END

THE SHATTERING

Daniele Bonfanti

1.

Now

The woman's face is beautiful, but it is the only part of her still intact.

She lies in an expanding puddle of her own blood on a grassy slope sprinkled with black ash, and a bearded, long-haired man kneels over her, his fine features upset, his right hand delicately caressing her hair as he holds her head in his left arm and repeats, "It's going to be all right, Thyya."

Their flamer-guns lie beside them on the ground, still hot, their muzzles sizzling and clicking against the burnt grass and charred earth around them; a hulk of a bald man and a petite redhead with a round face stand next to the couple, scanning around, weapons ready.

The redhead casts a quick look at the downed companion and spits, "Fucking rats."

Thyya looks like she's been nibbled by a thousand small mouths, and a thousand black filaments like long, badly ripped sutures pierce her body everywhere. She is wheezing in agony, and she laughs when, again, the bearded man assures her, *It's okay.*

"Yeah, sure, Berhault . . ." Her laughter turns into coughing, blood staining her peach-like lips and the creamy skin of her square, harmonious face. "You have to go now, we're close. You know, it may really be the last one, you…must."

Her head lolls back, and her eyes close.

"Thyya…" he whispers.

But the only answer is a thunder of crumbling ice from the brutal expanse of the Miage Glacier on the other side of the valley, its immense seracs climbing under the fangs of the Aguille Noire, a gigantic weapon drawn as if ready to deliver the splitting blow that will cut the world in two. Above everything, the summit prism of Mont Blanc watches, impassive. The whole sight is made of light as much as granite and ice.

A large, dark hand rests on the bearded man's shoulder. Berhault looks up to the huge, middle-aged, narrow-eyed man and just nods. Then he recovers his weapon and stands up in a graceful movement, trying his best to steel his quivering lips.

Guns in hands, pistols and knives swinging at their hips, they push on, quickly marching uphill in the dry air, permeated by a sweet, earthy fragrance. The exo-spines grafted to their backs sway as they walk—they all wear tank tops under the scorching high-altitude sun, and their backpacks wait for them down at their final two-minute stop at Lake Combal, at the base of the slope. Blue glyphs gleam on each carbon-titanium vertebra as the orphic marrow inside flows and bubbles. The spine goes down to their short tails, and up behind their necks in smaller sections. A ribbon-like collar engraved with symbols is connected to it. The exo-spine ends at their fontanels, where it sinks into their skulls.

"You guys really believe she was right? That it's the last one?" the redhead asks, drumming a march with her black nails on the tank of her glyph-carved weapon, an underslung canister mounted to the lower barrel.

Berhault is silent.

The mountain of muscles shrugs, "Well, her source was, how may we define it? Unconventional at best. For what we know, *we* may well be the last ones..." and he casts her a sideways look, *"Boss."*

She frowns, her black eyes widening between disturbingly long lashes. "What the...oh." She looks back at Thyya's corpse. "Really? Me?"

"Last time I checked your insignia..." he nods at the tattoos on her right shoulder.

Her gaze goes in search of Berhault—whose shoulder shows different tattoos: not their simple geometric codes, but beautiful, stylized goat-like antelopes, chamoix perhaps—maybe to ask for his opinion, but the slender man is looking forward, apparently indifferent to everything as he mindlessly puts one foot before the other. "C'mon, *technically*, but...I'm just a sarge, I assumed...I mean, both of you are way more experienced than me, and you've also actually seen one before."

"Berhault is a Runner, so you know as well as I he's outside the COC. And me, sorry, Boss, I'm just a grunt—I'm good at following orders and shooting things. And now, Pilar: I need you to stop whining and do your duty. Am I clear?" He looks her in the eye piercingly, and she snorts an odd smile that craters her moon face, stretching her thin upper lip over the full lower one.

"Fuck you, Gramps. And that's an order." Then she calls, "Berhault!"

He turns, but he doesn't seem to really see her.

"I need you to pull your shit together, Berhault. When we get to that ridge, it won't be a possessed pack, it won't be only rats and flies: it's the real deal. So Thyya's dead, and it sucks, but now quit that pathetic zombie act. And if we make it out of this alive, I'll personally blow you tonight to console you for your loss."

Berhault raises his angled eyebrows, and his blue eyes seem to come back from very far away as he almost manages a smile. "Yessir."

Berhault takes the lead; the behemoth looks at Pilar, nodding with an upturned smile and showing her his thumb.

Boots rustling on short grass and scraping on sparse stones. Aura of small flowers. The incline decreases.

And there: the ridge.

A man-tall pyramid of stones marks the pass.

The sight opens on the wide basin beyond. A crown of verdant mountains, rolling in gentle curves and baring spines of debris along the ridges, grooved by hollows gleaming with their eternal snowfields. In the bottom, an icy lake, deep blue, just like a frozen piece of sky fallen from above, its surface pierced by fang-like icebergs.

And the thing in the middle of it.

A huge creature, at least twenty meters tall. It appears to be made of black, thickly entangled filaments similar to those that mangled Thyya's body. A trunk or stem is rooted in the ice by a myriad of those filaments, many of which emerge and sink again in the ice and earth all around it, even hundreds of meters away, expanding underground like the mycelium of a fungus; high on the trunk, two thick limbs of filaments spread wide, making a cross; higher, a bulbous shape seethes with even more convoluted threads, like a skein; and from there, two bulky, bendy chitinous excrescences emerge much like bull horns.

Where the arms end, in a constantly waving bush of thinning filaments, vast swarms of flying specks burst out now; while the base of the trunk spews a horde of bigger snarls with tail-like things.

Pilar's eyes widen as she whispers, "How the fuck do we kill that?" while all swarms, no doubt, point to the trio on the ridge. Moving fast.

2.

Dadès Gorges Stronghold, post-Shattering Morocco – a year ago

"Everything you've been told throughout your life, until this moment, is a lie.

"Now, as you join the military, you get to know the truth we spare civilians and children.

"There's never been any WWIII; no fatal fallout. We're not down here just waiting for the air to clear up; to become breathable again. Actually, the air out there is much better now than thirty years ago."

The faces of boys and girls at attention show different emotions, but most of them slightly smirk at what must be some sort of initiation prank. But Thyya, on her platform, arms crossed behind the perfectly straight back of her black intelligence colonel uniform, goes on dead serious.

"There is another reason why you've been living down here for fourteen years.

"There _was_ a war. But it's not over as you've been told. And not one fought against humans."

The kids' faces grow paler. In her large, downturned hazel eyes there is no hint of a joke.

"Something happened twenty-five years ago, something we call _the Shattering_. Details will be for your science courses; as for now, just know that Gaia had been shielded by a field called the Veil, something that physicists noticed and defined only by its absence immediately after it was gone. Now we know it was a complex and invisible, geoengineering-generated bubble encircling our planet. We still don't know who put it there—or why they wanted to protect us. What we know is that our own despicable impact on the global ecosystem completely messed up that fine system.

"We screwed up, recruits. _Big time._

"When the Veil shattered, they found us, and they came.

"They've been looking for us for a long time, something like 150,000 years. Reason: unknown.

"During all that time, they probed, they reached out through Psi—which, as you've studied already in your classes, is the Universal Mind of which our species' Collective Mind is a fractal part. They felt us, tasted us, trying to understand us and, most important, to *locate us*. But they could not, as long as the Veil was in position.

"People who experienced contact with their minds were called *the possessed*. And they, the ones looking for us, were called *demons*.

"They have had a great many other names, but the one we use is the first one they had that we know of: *Anunnaki*.

"Their arrival was harbingered by insanity: with the Veil gone, the Anunnaki's influence could reach us so easily. Many humans were possessed, slaughtering families and friends and countless other people before killing themselves.

"Then, after *the Influence*, the Anunnaki came in the flesh, traveling aboard a comet: a large iceteroid they partially melted as fuel, seemingly out from somewhere in the Oort cloud—maybe their homeworld is there, we don't know.

"And they were greeted by our mass driver planetary defense system.

"Maybe they had underestimated us, maybe we were just lucky: their vessel was destroyed and most of them died. But not all of them: several managed to reach the surface of the planet, rooted themselves in strategic positions; and those were enough to crush us.

"They began with a concerted EMP emission, turning off power to most of the planet, an almost worldwide blackout which also killed, of course, advanced forms of communication.

"They had no weapons. They really did not need them when they could *manipulate* reality around them."

Voices buzz around the room. Aliens, they can swallow, but this...

3.

Barcelona, post-Shattering Catalunya – four months ago

A thermobaric warhead leaves the muzzle of the RPG on Gramps' shoulder, spreads its fins and flies, soaring over an uncannily still, silent Rambla.

It seems like the human statues had finally taken over, their army of monsters, freaks, and angels invading the long boulevard where grass, scrubs and even small trees have broken through the cobblestones—only they are really *too* still. And there is terror on their petrified, screaming faces.

The city has changed from the spicy cauldron of sounds and smells and movement it used to be pre-Shattering, before the Anunnaki Psi-strike. But it would be impossible not to recognize it.

It is as though Gaudí had come back from the grave with a vengeance, having indulged in too many mushrooms, his spirit seeping into every building, every wall, molding them to his will to create the architect's ultimate masterwork—the entire city a single mutated structure.

A different shape of how things could be.

There is not a single straight line; everything is frozen in a twisted and half-melted continuity, forms like faces or masks and corrugated backs, limbs, and shells extend from walls and roofs, parts of plants and animals and things that are both and neither. The Sagrada Familia must have infected the guts of the city, because its filigreed steeples burst from the cobblestones even here, as Casa Batlló and the other modernist buildings must have haunted their neighbors in a molding chain reaction: there are stone bones and fish scales, spiral turrets and giant lizards of polychrome porcelain climbing perspective-defeating vertical corridors, everything unmoving but seeming as though it's all just about to. The buildings are pierced by snaking galleries of terracotta-tree columns, leaning and scrubby with blade stones protruding.

Shattered things put together again; everything in the act of becoming something else.

Further, scattered around the city, the giant towers of the first century before the Shattering have grown tendrils and arms and faces of steel, glass, and concrete, and they are screaming to the sky they had once tried to touch.

And everything happened with people inside of them. They became part and raw material of the transformation. They can still be seen there.

The rocket meets the fourth storey of a building that looks like a coral reef, smashes through a skull-shaped window, and explodes as it strikes the wavy roof.

The foaming, yelling mob inside the room—about twenty men and women with ragged clothes and pieces of skin torn off all over their gaunt bodies, wildly rushing up a double-helix staircase—has just enough time to look up.

Then all the oxygen in the room is sucked in to feed the bomb, and the pressure wave tramples them, pulverizing the closer ones and slapping back like torn puppets the others among the crumbling rubble; then it is the sudden vacuum crushing their lungs to a pulp.

Only the last pair of them, which were still under cover below floor level, still moves after the explosion. They get up, stumbling on the warped steps, their eyes and ears bleeding, and their hands run up to their necks as they begin to choke.

They are lying still—fingers dug like claws in their throats and mouths open so wide they have torn where the lips meet—when Gramps arrives running up the stairs wearing a gas mask.

He quickly checks for movement among the litter of burning bodies, then begins to move the blocks of concrete obstructing the staircase. They almost seem light in his huge hands.

And up, as soon as there is a crevice to squeeze into.

Up two storeys more, fast.

A door opens on a diagonal tower on the roof, Gramps bursts out to see the aftermath of a desperate struggle.

On the far end of the flat roof, on the ground, lying with his back propped against the cast-iron balustrade, there is a soldier with a shotgun in his hands—its muzzle has twitched up to frame Gramps.

"Hey, son, I'm not one of them!" the big man smiles, raising his hands. "You boys gave them Possessed hell, well done," he adds, looking around at chimneys like crab pincers with many eyes, a multitude of bodies among them, sprawled on the ground, riddled with fresh holes, heads and limbs blown off. Five of them are lying around the soldier and one of them is a woman with the grip of his combat knife jutting out from the top of her head.

Three bodies are massacred soldiers still clutching their rifles.

The survivor is covered in scarlet and he is hacking blood.

Gramps is above him now, scrutinizing the young man's open belly. The intestines are out. He shakes his head, then sits beside the fizzling casualty, rummaging in his front pocket for a cigarillo. He offers it to the younger man, who grins. Gramps slides it between the soldier's lips and lights it with a match. The other one closes his eyes as he draws.

"Mission…accomplished. You'll find…safe houses…ammo and supplies…all the way from the Pyrenees to the Alps. Past Bourg St. Maurice…you're on your own." He burbles. "Maps. Right… pocket. Take them."

Gramps delicately pulls out a zip-locked plastic bag, with papers inside, from the soldier's pocket. "You did good. Sorry I was late to the rendezvous. Had a bit of trouble in Valencia: the whole city is swarming with rats. I was the only one to make it out alive." He lights up a cigarillo for himself. "You met anyone?"

"No," in a frail thread of voice. "Strongholds…Pont-du-Gard… Grenoble…gone."

Gramps nods and smokes in silence.

After the third draw, in the corner of his eye he sees the younger man's cigar dropping in his lap. He picks it up and extinguishes it.

He casts a look at the four casualties, shakes his head as he murmurs, "Let's hope the colonel's right about this."

The cigarillo is out. Gramps stands up, stuffs the maps and notes in his own pocket. Then he walks away.

4.

Now

The swarms are upon them. Pilar and Berhault just look in awe at the two clouds and the coming surge. The sheer presence of the Anunnaki, its majesty, annihilates their every reaction, turning them into quivering statues with useless guns.

A large shadow steps in before them, and from it a flaming cloud of ignited gas bursts up to meet the flies and cremate them—ash flakes whirling all around.

The gas-powered flame vanishes immediately as Gramps' thick, raw finger leaves the trigger to pull a secondary one, and a micro-grenade pops out from the over-slung launcher of his flamer-gun, its arc leading right into the middle-forward of the rat swarm that's coming up the snowfield, disintegrating them in an echoing explosion that melts the snow underneath.

The big man looks over his shoulder at his companions, his voice is strangely cool and soft, "Guys? Are you there?"

Pilar's black eyes are open wide as she shakes her head, as though waking from a dream. She nods, while Berhault answers by raising his flamer-gun and shooting the second swarm of flies, which Gramps is already doing.

Pilar dashes leftward, ordering, "Fan out! Gramps middle, Berhault right, ten meters apart!" and drops to a knee, joining the concert, serving a cluster of rats coming up from the snowy slope.

The things keep coming, and the three of them keep cooking and blasting them. All around torn filaments fly and sink, melting snow and ash into a sludge.

But something is off. Colors are not right. The sky shouldn't be violet and liquid; the boulders around should be firmer in their shape. Why are they warping like that?

The snow advances, spreading like the puddle of blood under Thyya's corpse, blades of ice slide on the wave front, rearing up taller and sharper, the whole thing climbing the slope toward them, a hungry entity ready to swallow. Crevasses open up, gaping, and they have no bottom.

The ice is coming to get Pilar, as she burns yet another clot of flies, all wrapped in cold sweat. A jackhammer working in her chest, her ears are raped by a continuous whistle.

She turns right while standing up and stumbling backward, screaming, "Fall back, the ice is coming!" But no Gramps there or Berhault beyond—just a boulder. Which was *not* there a moment ago. "*Gramps!*"

His voice, somewhere, to her *left*. Her name.

A few steps back, again, and she aims down at the ice mass closing in, within range of the dragon breath of her gun. Fire. And it melts. Too bad behind it there is a million-kilo ascending avalanche now, still coming. She just screams.

Gramps' shoulder is not gentle as it impacts hers, shoving her behind the boulder as the frozen tsunami hits the crest. Its roar is deafening as it breaks around the rock, and streams of snow cascade on them from above and both sides, but then it is gone and they are left coughing, trying to recover their breath.

"Are you okay?" he asks her as he opens the large arms that have sheltered her body, his back against the rock.

"I...I can't."

"Yes, you can. *Focus*. That thing must be tired after this one trick! We have to act now or...What the—"

Eyes opening in terror, bubbling noise, heat.

And he is sinking into a black magma, screaming.

Pilar's hands grasp his and pull, hard. Black, burnt flesh and acrid coils spread out. Gramps is half-embedded in the stone. She keeps pulling as she calls his name in desperation. His voice is crushing, squeezing into an unending *Nooo!* and now only his head and his jutting arms are out.

Berhault's voice, somewhere near: "Boss? Gramps!"

"*Here!*" she cries. "*Help me!*"

He runs on the dead avalanche, scrambling up on the ice cap it has formed behind the boulder, and finds her down that newborn cavern, trying to tear Gramps' huge frame—more than double her size—from the unyielding stone.

Berhault leaps down and grabs Gramps' other hand, joining the effort, but then the change is sudden.

The stone returns to stone.

Bones crack inside of it, their snapping reverberating through Gramps' hand and inside of both of them. His cry turns to a gargle.

His eyes swell, go red, shut off.

Their hands slide off the half-man, half-stone entity—like a modernist structure, like a human statue.

Berhault searches her eyes. She is bent on her knees, panting and crying, but her voice comes clear as she snarls, "*Let's...kill... that...fucker!*"

5.

Dadès Gorges Stronghold – a year ago

Thyya waits, unmoving, and her silence subdues the recruits' buzz. All stares on her, she begins pacing and talking again.

"You've studied that reality is unstable, fleeting, and that it's our perceiving it that defines it. No doubt you've chalked it up to abstract theory—I know I did, at your age. But it's not abstraction at all. We literally project reality, translating it from thoughts inside of Psi. Well, the Anunnaki are so different from us that their translation is a very different one—but what they can do is, inside certain limits, *choose* how to translate. We could, too, potentially, but we don't know how. And it appears they can impose their version on ours.

"That's what they did. Relatively small changes, huge butterfly effects.

"For a while, analogic radios kept working. In those days we heard what was happening all around the world: earthquakes, tsunamis, volcanic eruptions, tornadoes…the deadliest days of humankind, the days in which we understood that we'd been living with a loaded gun aimed at our collective temple for so many years. The Anunnaki knew how to pull the trigger.

"Entire continents were wiped out in a few days.

"And there were other, stranger things—you'll learn about Psi-strikes.

"But we fought back. And killed them, losing armies in the effort, but, in the end, there were not enough of them to continue that kind of global onslaught. Their attacks became sparser, while their few survivors went into hiding.

"Then radios, too, went dark, and there was a great silence.

"In the eerie quiet, we began to organize ourselves.

"We had discovered, by then, that we *knew things* about them. They've been in our minds forever, but this connection went both ways—to misquote Nietzsche: if the Abyss looks into you, you got a pretty look-see yourself into the Abyss. Fact is, we didn't *know* what that sight was and we called it many names: genius, epiphany, madness, illumination, vision, miracle, witchcraft, apparition, or we simply couldn't make sense of it—like Bronze Age calendars calibrated on axis precession...But all throughout history, thousands of pages were written about the Anunnaki, under the subconscious disguise of myth and esoteric texts.

"And that's why we *recognized* them the first day they arrived.

"Seventeenth century alchemist-scientists like Isaac Newton talked about *Prisca Sapientia*—the lost, ancient science they were trying to *re*discover. Turns out it wasn't lost in time, but in space. It was in the minds of the ones probing us. We absorbed scraps, and it took centuries. But now we were ready to put those scraps together.

"Cryptologists like myself were born: scholars dedicated to the study of those ancient texts, now really understanding their secret meaning and looking into them for keys to understand their weaknesses.

"With that knowledge, now conscious and decoded, and modern means, we came up with ways to protect us from their influence. We created a new tech rooted in millennia-old secrets.

"We augmented our soldiers with it. Maybe some of you are looking forward to the enhancements, to the exo-spines you've seen, thinking they will make you stronger. Well, they will (though I can assure, you'll regret that desire while they're being grafted into your vertebrae), but their main function is another: in fact, the exo-spine is primarily a reality-stabilizing device.

"And we built the underground Strongholds like the one you live in, keeping together a phantom of civilization thanks to a network of highly trained Runners physically moving information between them.

"Places protected by glyphs engraved in stone, and railguns."

6.

Cadiz, post-Shattering Spain – five months ago

"Is there any water?"

"Oh, by all means, there's a lot," Berhault answers with a grin over his shoulder, looking at Thyya's exhausted face behind him. His right hand leaves the paddle to perform a theatrical gesture to the expanse of blue around them. "This is the Atlantic."

"Fuck," she coughs, "you, Berhault."

His free hand rummages between his legs in the bobbing kayak cockpit and reaches back to her, offering a red canteen. "Here, my last drops, make them count."

Her tongue slides along parched lips. "Thank you." A short, measured sip, her eyes closed in near ecstasy under her thin, arching eyebrows at the touch of wetness. A throat-clearing cough. Slouching on the backseat, her paddle strapped with bungees to the deck beyond her, Thyya looks at the coastline a hundred meters starboard, rolling dunes lighting up with orange and gold in the late-afternoon Andalusian sky; sparse bushes sucking in greens. "How soon?"

"Almost there."

An acid laugh. "You said that *before dawn*, you know?"

"Well, at dawn we *were* almost there…"

Her big, downturned eyes were half-closed: now they open wide and become even bigger. "*What?!*"

"…almost across the strait. Almost reached Europe." He turns, looking ahead; restarts paddling. She cannot see his impish grin. "Wasn't that what you were asking, honey?"

"*Honey?*" Then the weight of her eyelids wins over her rage, and her back seems to go purée. She slurs, "You fucking Runners, you think you're above everything and everyone, right? It's all a big joke to you, ha? You better show some respect."

Berhault stops paddling and turns back. His clear cerulean eyes are blades pointed on her. "*Colonel*, I think you should appreciate the fact that I'm restraining myself, here. I'm awfully tempted to drop you in the drink and see how good a swimmer you are, cryptologist or not. After the kind of fuck-up you're responsible for, maybe it would do my Karma some good."

Thyya just looks at him in silence, her gaze firm. Then she whispers, "It was a risk worth taking."

"Two thousand people."

"I know that number very well, Berhault."

"The whole Dadès Gorge Stronghold—*gone*. It was a miracle I managed to pull you out of that hell, and maybe I should have left you to the Possessed. I'm sure those people would have been happy to talk to you about what you'd done. Surely, they would have agreed if you told them what you had in that hangar of yours—what you'd secretly brought in and kept inside that freezer just under their feet. Why not?"

"It was a top-secret operation. They didn't *need* to know. You have to try and know things about your enemy if you want to have a fighting chance. This is war, Berhault, we're not playing games."

"Really? You weren't playing with your friend the *fucking Anunnaki head* down there? So, tell me, what is this incredibly effective knowledge you extracted with your fancy *interrogation* that was worth the whole Stronghold?"

"It *was* worth it. I can only say this to you; let me talk with Commander Santacruz in San Sebastián and—"

"Bullshit, Thyya." She slightly frowns at her first name from his mouth—while an electric thrill runs up her spine—but stays silent. "It's all bullshit. You killed all those people because you cryptologists like to play God."

His eyes stone hers, and that gaze lasts forever, until he turns, his paddle striking the water like it's personal.

"I'll tell you," she murmurs. The paddle stops mid-air. "So maybe you'll forgive me, even if I cannot forgive myself."

***

"The interrogation *worked*. Through the Psi-link, we were able to interpret scraps of its memory.

"I know *why* they've been looking for us. I know *why* the Veil was created and *by whom*.

"We had a theory the Anunnaki had been here before, and that they did something to us at a genetic level; it was supported by extensive mythological and archeo-astronomical evidence from all around the world.

"Now we know. A rogue group of them was here. 150,000 years ago. We would call them…scientists as well as priests. They had discovered a great secret, about the very principles of nature. Something that their mainstream creed deemed as blasphemy. The secret of Ascension, of melding their whole collective mind with Psi, becoming one with the Universe. This clashed hard with their religion, so the members of that group were condemned as heretics, and they fled their planet, Nibiru. They reached Gaia, where they hid the secret, encoding it in human DNA—in the strands we call *junk DNA*, the ones we thought useless 'cause they don't code for anything. In the process, the human race was uplifted to a higher level of consciousness and *programmed* to rediscover the secret hidden inside of itself, at a due time, when ready to understand it. The rogue Anunnaki geo-engineered Gaia to create the Veil, hiding it from Nibiru, as they perfectly knew the rest of their kind would have come to eradicate us—think of it: we are blasphemy incarnate. They were unprepared for the alien environment, though, and rapidly succumbed to Earth bacteria. I think you know the rest of the story…"

***

Berhault's face is vibrating with fury, his lips quiver, he looks as if he's about to snap her head off with a bite. "And *this pile of shit* is the reason two thousand people died back there? How *the fuck* does this help us fight them?"

"This is fundamental knowledge about our foe's motives, and—"

"Bullshit!" But he seems to spot something in her eyes, a glint. "There's more, right?"

Thyya sighs. "Yes. There's a last piece of information, the most important piece. And it's simple." She squints. "And *useful.*"

Berhault is waiting. The ocean is silent, as he is, just roaring somewhere in the distance.

"The Anunnaki are all in contact through Psi; we knew that, of course. Well, the one I interrogated, it was in contact with just one other."

Berhault's forehead produces a straight, deep wrinkle. "If they are all in contact, why just the o..." his mouth freezes on the vowel as it hits him.

"Because there is no longer any other." She slowly nods, letting the sheer size of the information sink in, then she adds, businesslike: "And I know where it is."

***

Her pupils fix on the muscles of his back, hypnotically darting as his torso swivels at each stroke, and the tattooed chamoix leap on those boulders of flesh out of the cover of his curly hair, and then slip back in. "Have you even slept?"

He shakes his head just enough for her to see. His skin smells like leather.

And then she must have dozed off herself, because Cadiz is in sight when she opens her eyes again, bright white and pastel flat-roofed houses under a sky that looks broken in two—flaming to the left of the citadel, deepening on the right. Cobalt waves shatter against the breakwaters under the cathedral, its walls and twin domes seized by creepers.

A thin, long finger of land reaches out into the ocean, and on a rocky islet bordered by tidal pools at its point, the fortress at the end of the world—the castle of San Sebastián waits for them.

The tip of the iceberg of the Stronghold beneath.

***

Pilar comes out of a steel door in the castle—the outer walls all inscribed in huge blue glyphs with smaller symbols encircling the mouths of cannons—her rifle casually slung in military patrol carry, strutting ahead with a full-toothed grin while Berhault disembarks and hauls up Thyya, holding her worn-out, semi-unconscious body, like a newly married husband with his wife.

"Welcome, Runner! Hell, you're the first one we've seen in two years. We were beginning to think we were the last…" She frowns as her black eyes frame the insignia tattooed on Thyya's shoulder. Her formidable lashes fanning air twice. Then she shakes her head and straightens up at attention, awkwardly saluting. "Colonel?"

Thyya's head lolls sideways, but her eyes cannot seem to put into focus the soldier, who, without waiting for an order, drops her salute and breaks her stance to quickly offer a canteen. Thyya looks at a vague point beyond her, as her tongue struggles to scratch out some words, "I need to speak with Commander Santacruz."

"Colonel's dead, sir. I'll bring you to Major Torres. I'm sorry to report San Sebastián is down to only thirty-three people."

"What happened?" asks Berhault while gently pouring water into Thyya's parted lips.

"We had flies."

***

7.

Long strides in plumes of white, weapons high, Pilar and Berhault run down the slope, side by side, leaving behind the boulder which, now, is also Gramps.

The Anunnaki looks idle. No flies, no rats swarming from it.

"It can't be long before it recovers!" Pilar urges. "As we hit the bottom, you go right, I go left, close in on it together. Clear?"

Berhault does not answer.

"Berhault?"

He shakes his head. "Yessir." Absent. Distant. Slow.

A shiver through her.

Pilar deliberately loses a few steps and looks at his back: the glyphs on his exo-vertebrae gleam orange.

"Berhault! Stop and go back, you're being broken! Go back and stop thinking about Thyya!"

Too late: red. He turns, leaps, has his knife in his hand already and he is just too quick. Blood squirts from Pilar's arm, just a couple centimeters safe of her brachial artery, drawing a crescent in the snow.

He is upon her, a knee on her neck. The blade glistens.

A back thrust, exploiting gravity and incline, unbalances him; Pilar is on her feet again, gasping. But he is as well, and already pouncing on her like a puma.

She pivots on her right foot, turning ninety degrees counterclockwise and bracing her left foot in the snow. She grabs the front of Berhault's tank top with her left hand, and slightly ducking, her right arm slides under his torso, loading his weight on her shoulder; exploiting his own momentum, she pushes with her legs and he flies and flips in the air before going down hard, face first.

Pilar draws her pistol and shoots, but the two bullets just open holes in the snow; Berhault has rolled aside and now he jumps at her again—his face a mask of his true one, eyes lost, mouth gaping and foaming in a scratching yell.

She shoots him in the chest.

He grabs her neck with talon-like hands, his blood sputtering on her breasts, tongue thrust close to her face from his primal maw.

His grip is inhumanly strong, but it only lasts a second—enough to break her neck had it not been augmented.

He blinks, his features relax. For an instant, he is Berhault again and he smiles at her and they seem two lovers about to kiss.

He slouches, sliding down her.

Pilar swallows, holstering her pistol.

Then, her quivering hand slowly rises behind her neck. Her fingertips brush her implants. Wet. Oily.

His grasp must have partially torn them.

She closes her eyes as she moves the hand before her face. Lids are forced open by reluctant muscles. The orphic marrow on her fingers is glowing orange.

8.

Dadès Gorges Stronghold – a year ago

"And now it's twenty-five years since the Shattering.

"We still don't know why they attacked us.

"The few of us have been battling the few of them—and their rats and flies and Possessed thralls.

"Hunting them down 'til we find the last one, or the last one of us is slain.

"This is what we do. What you're going to do. This is what you'll be fighting for.

"Your training begins today."

9.

San Sebastián Stronghold – two thousand kilometers ago

"I was a child, then, these were the dungeons of the old castle, I was afraid and you held my hand.

"I asked you where Mommy was. And you told me she was out fighting demons."

Sitting in the lotus position, Pilar's eyes fix the photo on a small shrine set in the rocky wall. A necklace with a small lapis pendant adorns the frame, and a bunny made of rags slouches against its base. A man smiles from the picture. The resemblance is unmistakable: same round face and red hair, same generous lower lip and black eyes.

"Well, Dad, tomorrow I leave. To fight demons, too. Guess she'd be proud, right?

"And listen to this: Colonel Stick-Up-Her-Butt says the mission we're leaving for is something of a showdown. We're down to four in the Stronghold after the fucking flu three months ago and the attack last month; so we're all going, of course. We're double-locking San Sebastián and hope to find it still standing when—I know: if—we make it back. She says it's the last one. She's nuts, by the way. But what the hell, it's not as though we had a lot of choice.

"We must go all the way to the Alps. Four comrades gave their lives to set up safe houses for us along the way, so we really cannot let them down, right?

"But maybe you're thinking it's pointless anyway...I mean: we could actually be the last people on Gaia. Even if we kill it, the four of us could hardly repopulate the planet (though I must confess, Dad, I wouldn't mind at all repopulating with Berhault—hope Her Majesty doesn't hear me, she definitely has a thing for him).

"But Gramps says there used to be tech to artificially reproduce, pre-Shattering; that we could recover it. And Colonel Long Legs also

says there were places where frozen, fertilized human eggs were stocked, and maybe those are still there.

"Whatever.

"We go, we kill it, then we'll see."

10.

Now

Pilar screams.

There is a hive of wasps in her head, buzzing and *stinging.*

It is the Anunnaki's voice, breaking through her failing exospine, calling.

And it burns.

"Out. Of. My. Fucking. *Head!*"

And she starts running, leaving Berhault's corpse behind in the snow.

Warm blood on hot skin, her gashed arm pulsates, tingling. Freezing orphic marrow, trickling down her nape, along her sweaty back.

A geyser erupts just before Pilar; she twists around to dodge it, falling and scrambling back to her feet. A necklace of snow bursts around her. The sky is black, hail slamming her from all directions. The snow moans loudly.

Pilar unleashes a battle cry of rage amidst the din of wind and ice.

She hits the grassy bottom of the valley, and the space separating her from the shape of the Anunnaki, half-seen in the gale, suddenly compresses—or maybe it was dilated before.

The alien rises from the frozen lake, just fifty meters away. Its filaments wildly whirl and wiggle, its head throbs fast, a black stain in the white inferno. A low vibration through the shriek of the wind: it is coming from the creature.

Forward, head down to face the wind.

Every step is a torture. Her muscles are shards of broken wood biting into themselves.

Filaments emerge everywhere, like lengths of roots arcing briefly out of the ground—but now tips of them, too, burst out of the earth, on her right, rearing up and striking like faceless cobras.

Pilar dodges left, avoiding two, half-turning to drop a grenade and clear a swathe, and runs just in time to avoid an assault from behind; she darts through the corridor of wavering black snakes that close in on both sides and keep jabbing, more than one of them hitting her.

But she keeps going, ribbons of blood trailing behind her and tracing crimson arabesques in the wind.

She is close, stepping on the frozen lake, but everything around is falling apart and it is difficult to recognize things. There is its reality, superimposing on the known one.

Pilar's mind struggles to give meaning to stimuli coming from extraneous senses, to collocate them in usual patterns. Unaided by the failing exo-spine, it is giving up . . .

Feeling the gravity of the mountains, the mountains as gravity; waves and radiation braiding in the sky, electricity brewing in what must be clouds, the dance and mating of molecules, decay, creation, all things between, below, the murmuring stream of geomagnetism and many other forces with no name flowing like blood in the vessels of Gaia. Feeling the planet spinning.

No matter. Energy.

Nothing is ever real.

Everything is becoming something else.

And could become anything.

The Anunnaki is an ascending white flame, throbbing in an ultraviolet spiral well.

It is clear, now: the reason it has chosen this place, this temple, this node. Undercurrents converging. Here. Now.

It all can be changed.

Eyelids close. Air flows down hot, slow, opening lungs. A single heartbeat. Two. As her eyes open, everything spins frozen around her and silence has fallen—has always been there.

A distant sound like a slow choir: four slow chords, ascending melody—the soprano notes *C, D, F*—and descending harmony.

It is inside. Buried deep in DNA.

The voice of all things, as one.

The fourth and last note is of things shattering—

And Pilar screams, and her eyes are black fire as the orphic marrow in her exo-spine burst out scarlet, her scream a lance of synesthetic negentropy piercing walls, opening a narrow fissure through which the Anunnaki can be seen again, in the middle of the shifting colors—many of them inexistent, but probable.

She is standing at its very base. A tiny thing before the figure.

She shoots.

She empties the magazine of her grenade launcher in its head—spurts of fluid splutter about in high hisses as her own blood and marrow drip down on the ice—and then she squeezes the trigger of the flamer and keeps it there, engulfing the trunk in fire; the layers of ice beneath sublimate in flourishes of vapor as the creature slowly begins sinking, while gelid water overflows and spreads over the thick surface, reaching her boots and drenching them and washing the red away.

The wide nozzle sputters a last cough of flame.

She drops the weapon on the melting ice and empties the pistol's magazine in the burning tangle that wildly writhes as though dancing to the sound of the collective agonizing cry—too distant to be heard up here—of countless possessed people, dying with it.

Then she runs in the whirling panorama where holes more dark than black open, swallowing pieces of landscape all around; just running forward.

Hitting the snowy slope, she feels snow and sees white. *White, focus on the white.* Run.

Ascending the avalanche, to the ridge. A red trail soaking the snow.

Only then she looks back—the alien is collapsing its last filaments into the water and onto the surrounding ice, rotting already.

Tears fill Pilar's eyes; she lets them flow.

Then looks at Mont Blanc.

The mountain laid upon all the other mountains.

She keeps dragging up her gaze and it keeps being there, where open sky should be; following up the pronged tongue of ice that descends from the hanging granite pillars of the summit prism, its shoulders extending from one side to the other of the horizon, making distances and sizes incomprehensible.

"You don't care, right?" she asks, her voice broken in sobs, her body covered in blood, mud, snow, and sweat.

But the god of granite, ice, and light does not answer. He never does.

"You can't give a shit about all this, about these last one-hundred-thousand years. About us. About them. We were just passing by, right? And now maybe I'm the last person on Earth." She laughs, just a touch hysterical. "Well, good, no one will come disturb me."

Then she sits on a rock and looks at the mountain.

END

LABYRINTH

William Meikle

I always wondered why she needed a three-man bodyguard team; over time I came to realize it gave her more opportunities for doing what she did best, that is winding men around her little finger. It always felt like overkill to have a trio of former British Army squaddies, fully tooled up, just standing around on deck as the yacht visited the fleshpots, casinos and rich-folks' playgrounds of the Med. But as a Sheik's wife she had an image to protect, even if she was still at heart a Karen from the King's Road in Chelsea who'd slept her way to a fortune. Still, the pay was better than good, and protect is what we did best.

To tell the truth it was a cushy number for the first six months, swanning around the Med, looking hard when we needed to, and doing the rounds of some pretty upmarket bars and clubs on our nights off. A lot of the time we felt like spare dicks at an orgy. But the trouble, when it finally came, made me all too happy that there were three of us on the job. And I also had reason to be thankful for the Sheik; we didn't see much of him, but he took care of his 'investments'... there was an emergency locker in the dinghy we were in with enough firepower stowed away to start a war.

It turned out we needed it.

That trouble I was mentioning started when Her Majesty decided she wanted to do some skinny-dipping and sunbathe on a secluded beach. Of course, any old beach wouldn't do, it had to be one to her very specific liking, so we sailed for days, trawling a chain of islands between Crete and mainland Greece before she found her spot. Then she took to the dinghy with the three of us along, 'in case of trouble' she said, although we all knew we were going to get a 'look but don't touch' view of all that wasn't on offer.

It went as expected at first.

She showed us her tits, teased us with a towel that she'd show more, then went for a swim while we got a pot of coffee brewing on the camp stove. She eventually got out of the water further along the beach, just far enough that we could see her, not far enough to see everything.

John passed round the smokes and in the seconds between me leaning in for a light and moving backwards again she was gone. I caught a glimpse of something big heading off at speed into the cliffy section above the sand but by the time I reached the spot there was just her towel and a load of scuff-marks and footprints I couldn't make any sense of. John and Dave wanted to head off into the passageway in the rocks, but I had to hold them back.

"No. We go in tooled up or not at all. Anybody desperate enough to snatch her in daylight like this won't think twice about putting us down."

It took two minutes to get back to the dinghy and ransack the emergency locker. We were all in her demanded clothing; white shirts, black slacks and rubber deck shoes; none of that could be helped. But at least we got a flak jacket, an automatic rifle and several mags each from the locker. We hooked up three stun grenades each, I strapped a diving knife to my ankle and we were back again at her discarded towel in the sand minutes later.

It already felt too late.

The scuffed marks led in a trail into the rocks below the cliffs, a tumbled area of large boulders that had come down from above in ages past and formed a natural, high walled passageway which cast us in deep shadow as I took the lead and we headed in.

We moved quietly, hoping to hear a cry from Her Majesty, but the only sound was the soft scuff of our feet on sand. And even that was lost after a few yards when the ground underfoot became solid rock. Something tickled my nasal passages, a smell I couldn't quite identify, musty and thick, like a heady perfume applied by a woman with a heavy hand. There were no branches off the trail, which was just as well, for there were no clues as to the whereabouts of our employer.

I expected to have to climb up the cliffs away from the shore in pursuit of the abductors so was surprised when the passage led directly to the mouth of what appeared to be a large cave, and not a natural one at that for there was clear evidence of working around the entrance and the ground leading inside was composed of rectangular slabs fitted into a formal pathway.

"What the fuck is this now, Sarge?" Dave asked, but I had no answer for him. I switched on the light on my rifle and stepped inside.

***

There was more evidence inside the entrance that the cave was in fact a man-made tunnel; the walls were lined with large, tightly fitted blocks of stone. I've been in chambered tombs in other parts of the world and this place gave off the same sense of great age. But what these had lacked, and this place had in spades, was a sense that it was still in use. For one thing the smell I'd already noted was thicker now and could be tasted in the mouth as well as smelled. The floor was dotted with splatters of blood; I had a bad moment until I realized these were old, well, at least older than today. I was starting to think that the abductor we were after might be an animal rather than man, but for the life of me I couldn't think of any predator here in the Med that might fit the bill.

I was still pondering that when a scream, Her Majesty, in some pain, echoed down to us from somewhere deeper inside. I put on a spurt of speed but had to stop after only five paces when faced with two tunnels, one left, one right.

"Split up, Sarge?" John said.

"Aye, that's a great fucking idea," I replied. "Have you never seen a film, lad? No, we stay as a team. This way."

I went left on a mental toss of a coin. After five yards we came to another left/right junction. I went left again and almost immediately hit a dead end. I was starting to get an idea what we were up against.

"It's a fucking maze, Sarge," Dave said.

"No shit, Sherlock?"

I backed us out to the turning, took out my knife and made a horizontal score on the wall at eye level. It showed up as a white line against the darker rock in my sight-light.

"This means we've been this way already," I said.

I went right and met another dead end almost immediately. I backed us out to the junction then backed out again to the first decision point. I scored a large plus sign on the wall by the left entrance.

"And this means do not, under any circumstances, be fucking stupid enough to go this way again. Kapeesh?"

I got a nod from both of them just as another scream came from inside.

We went right.

***

The first attack came at us so fast I didn't know what had happened until it was over. We'd reached a junction, I was putting a horizontal line at the mouth of the passageway that we'd just come out of when a bulky figure came out of the right hand tunnel ahead of us. I got my rifle up enough to light up a pair of dark-skinned, muscular legs, then something huge hit me, hard, like a rugby tackle from a solid prop and I went down, my gun light showing only the bare ground. Two seconds later Dave screamed in pain, somebody let off two quick shots that rang like thunder in my ear. I heard heavy footsteps echo away down the corridor to the left, then the only sound was Dave, whimpering.

I went over to him while John took guard. I shone my light in his face. It was pale, almost white, his eyes black holes in the shadows. He spoke and it was obvious he was in some pain.

"Fucker stabbed me, Sarge," he said. "Got me a good one too."

I shifted my light down. There was blood at his waist, a lot of it. I helped him shuck out of the flak jacket and peeled his soaked shirt aside. The wound was almost the size of my fist, a hole that had been punched into him just above his left hip and one that was still oozing blood. Between us we got it stuffed with most of his shirt and got him to his feet.

"Can you walk, man?"

He grimaced, but nodded.

"Get back outside...follow the horizontal lines at each junction and they'll lead you out. There's a first aid kit in the dinghy. Patch yourself up as best you can. If anything comes out that isn't us or Her Majesty, blow it to fuck."

"Sounds like a plan, Sarge," he said.

I patted him on the shoulder as he turned away.

"See you in ten," I replied, then he was gone back down the corridor.

"Fuck me, Sarge," John said. "What made a wound like that?"

"Sword, maybe?" I answered. "I just don't know. Let's go and see if we can find out. We need to give that fucker a lesson in manners."

***

I had a choice to make; left after our attacker, or right, where he'd come from. I went right, assuming that, if he'd also been the abductor of Her Majesty, he might have her stashed away somewhere in that direction. We moved more carefully now, with me lighting the way ahead, John watching our backs and making sure we marked every passageway exit we passed.

My gut feeling was that we were getting ever deeper under the cliffs, descending slightly as we went. The air got thicker, the smell—now a stench—even more pronounced. There was no repeat of Her Majesty's screaming, and I wasn't sure if that was good or bad...I would have welcomed some noise right then.

My only plan was to go right when I could. It was working so far in that we hadn't yet come back to any junctions we'd visited before, but I was only too aware of the passage of time; there wasn't just Her Majesty to be thinking of. There was Dave too, out on the beach, hopefully, and wounded God knew how badly. My worry was that he'd bleed out before we got him to help.

"Faster," I whispered, and moved in deeper.

Soon after that we started to see faint light ahead. We killed our sight lights and crept forward. I didn't blame John for not maintaining silence; it was all I could do to stop myself from joining him.

"Fuck me," he whispered. It lacked something in descriptive quality, but it certainly covered my own feelings on the matter. We stood in an entranceway looking across a high domed chamber that gleamed, brilliant white, with marbled pillars and high arches in the Ancient Greek style rising up and away high above to where a soft light permeated through from a crevasse in the cliff. Seven other entrances showed as darker semicircles almost equally spaced around the outer rim of the chamber. There was no sign of Her Majesty. A small waterfall cascaded down into a pool in the chamber's center sending a rainbow dancing. And yet, despite the wonders of the building, that wasn't what had brought John's exclamation to his lips.

No, that would have been the things that slept scattered about the steps around the small wall that enclosed the pool.

The more classically minded of you will have guessed already; even a relative illiterate like me had heard that story. Everybody knows what lives in mazes on Greek islands. I saw them, I just wasn't ready to believe in them yet. They all looked to be around six-foot tall or even a tad larger. Below mid-chest they were built like a stocky man, chunky, heavily muscled, and solid as a brick shithouse... and completely naked. Hands and feet looked human, but on the large side. Above nipple level they were bull, complete with flaring nostrils, a hairy black mane and high curving horns, the sharp points rising in a crescent above their heavy brows. At least I now knew what kind of weapon had pierced Dave's side and, looking at these, I knew he was lucky he hadn't been run all the way through. I was still trying to process what I was seeing when John pulled me backward into the corridor.

"She's not here," he whispered. "We should double back."

I saw the same fear in his eyes that was beginning to eat at me. But Her Majesty was in here somewhere and I was getting paid to keep her out of trouble. Duty called and I answered.

"Go back? No way. We've already been that way. My guess is she's in one of the other rooms off the chamber. We need to search them."

"Aye? Good luck with that, Sarge. How do you suggest we get round those things?"

"We don't go round. We go through," I said, and showed him my rifle. He went as white as Dave had been earlier.

"I'm not sure I can do that, Sarge."

The decision became a moot one seconds later when another scream, recognizably a woman's, echoed around us. Hoarse bellowing answered from within the chamber.

"Showtime," I said and stepped into the entrance way.

***

They were faster than I expected they'd be.

The first one saw me as it was rising from the steps, turned, bellowed and launched into a head-down careering run coming straight at me. I put two shots between its eyes but it took its time realizing it was dead and I had to step back to avoid it before it eventually fell in a heap at my feet. By that time, the other three had risen and were similarly coming at us. My next shots were rushed, missing their mark. John at my side had more luck although he wasn't trying to be as precise as I, spraying a volley in a wide arc that sent a line of red holes across the great chest of another of the beasts, knocking it to the ground and allowing John a clear line of sight to the one behind it. His second volley turned that one's head to mush and it too was dead before it hit the ground.

I had troubles of my own. As I said, my shots had gone wide. That left a gap for the last of the four Minotaur to get at me and I wasn't going to get time for another shot; I tried to side-step out of its path but tripped on its dead brother at my feet. Then it was on me. It felt like I was being smothered under a ton of hot flesh. It lowered its head, horns seeking to pierce me somewhere around the heart. It was just by sheer luck that I was able to get the rifle barrel up under its left armpit.

I pulled the trigger and kept firing until the weight fell away. When I stood, I was soaked head to toe in warm blood and the thing at my feet wasn't much more than a wet piece of flesh, bone and more blood.

More hoarse bellows echoed around us.

"There's more of these buggers?" John said.

Another voice split the air.

"Andy!"

It was Her Majesty. I looked up to see her in the entranceway directly across the chamber from me. She was as naked as the day she was born but in no state to worry about her modesty. When she went to run forward towards me another Minotaur came out of the entrance behind her. This one was bigger, half as big again as the ones I'd just killed, horns almost scraping the arched roof above it, its huge chest and belly a mass of white scar tissue, the great mane almost full gray. It grabbed at the woman, pulling her tight against itself, looked directly at me and let out a roar. It was answered by more bellowing from the other entranceways. The old one turned and dragged Her Majesty away into the darkness.

I slammed a fresh, if somewhat bloody, mag into my rifle.

"We're going to have company," I shouted to John. "Cover me."

Without waiting for a reply, I set off at a run across the chamber.

***

John's first shots echoed thunder all around me as I ran. I went past the waterfall and pool at full pelt, half expecting to be attacked at any moment, but it seemed that the big one was more intent on getting away with Her Majesty than anything else and John was doing a fine job of giving me cover. I reached the entranceway without being gored and immediately made my way inside, switching on my rifle's light as I went.

Within a few steps I came to a junction. I kept to the plan and went right, finding myself standing above a large and ever widening pit. Things moved down there and when I pointed my light down I saw what I at first took to be more Minotaur then realized it was a small herd of closely-packed cattle. I took it for the Minotaurs' pantry...they had to eat something after all, and I didn't have time for further conjecture. I backed out to the junction and went left.

I found them two junctions later in a large cave. The end of the line. It was lit by several small oil lamps high on ledges and lined with what looked to be goat skins and possibly seal pelts. A pile of cleaned white bones made a pyramid in the corner but my gaze was firmly on the Minotaur. It stood in the center of the chamber, clasping Her Majesty to its chest. A pair of fiery-red eyes like hot coals embedded in the skull glared at me.

I showed him the rifle. He knew what it was clearly enough and tugged the woman tighter to him. To my astonishment he spoke, although I didn't understand the word.

"Kunaja," he said, and repeated it louder.

I didn't have time for conversation. I sent a volley into the pile of bones, scattering white fragments everywhere to get him imagining what such a volley would do to his innards, then mimed that he should let the woman go.

He didn't show any signs of complying. Lucky for me Her Majesty had ideas of her own on that account. She was exactly the right height compared to him for the action she took; she pistoned her right elbow back, *hard*, hitting the largest set of cock and balls you'd ever wish to see dead-center. The yelp of outraged pain from the Minotaur was the most human thing I saw from it.

Her Majesty wriggled out of his arms and ran for me. At the same time, I unhooked one of the stun grenades, primed it and lobbed it in the beast's general direction. The woman's warm hand nestled into mine a few moments later and together we fled as the corridor blazed and boomed in white noise behind us.

***

We hit the chamber with the pool and waterfall at a dead run, the bellows of the big lad roaring in our ears from somewhere not too distant behind us. The chamber had gone from a marvel of marble to a charnel house in the short time I'd been away. John was still in the doorway immediately opposite with a heap of dead Minotaur, a score and more, lying between us and him. The whole place stank of blood, pish and shit.

"I was just about to give up on you when I heard the bang," he shouted. "I've got them running scared away back to their holes for now. Can we please get the fuck out of here?"

"Happy to oblige," I said.

As we reached his side and stopped, just for long enough for me to get my shirt off and allow Her Majesty to regain at least a modicum of modesty, the big Minotaur arrived in the archway opposite. It stopped and stared in obvious astonishment at the carpet of its dead.

The moan of anguish that came from it was almost as human as the pained howl I'd heard back in its bedchamber. Once again, it turned its gaze on me and it was fury I now saw in those great red eyes.

John and I had the same idea; we both primed stun grenades and tossed them into the chamber. Then, with Her Majesty once again grabbing tight at my hand, we legged it out of there fast as the passageway went white and loud behind us.

***

The escape in the dark was a nightmarish one. The bellows of angry Minotaur echoed loud behind us and at every turn we expected to run into more of them. The only plus point was the fact that my markings on the wall showed up clear and white and we didn't make any false moves, but by the time we saw daylight and the exit ahead, the roaring from our pursuers sounded far too close for comfort at our heels. I was all too aware of the expanse of open sand that we would have to cover to reach the dinghy. My hope was that Dave was still *compos mentis* and with it enough to give us some cover… otherwise it was going to be a hard road to take.

When we reached the entrance we stopped again, just long enough to prime the remaining stun grenades and roll them back into the darkness. We were already off and away across the hot sand, squinting in the sudden brightness of the sun, when the booming roar of them going off reverberated along the side of the cliffs to our left.

Dave, God bless the lad, had the dinghy at the edge of the water and was lying in it with his rifle aimed in our direction.

"Come on, you lazy buggers," he shouted. "I've got you covered. Move your arses."

We moved our arses. Not quite fast enough though, for before we were halfway to the dinghy Dave sent two shots whizzing past us.

"They're coming," he shouted. "Too many for me to take."

I thrust Her Majesty behind me and dropped to my belly, already taking aim. John did the same at my side and I was pleased to note that the woman had sense to join us and get out of Dave's line of fire.

A dozen Minotaur were barreling their way along the beach towards us, the big old one bringing up the rear, its bellowing roars now driving the others forward.

They ran right into a shooting gallery and it wasn't much of a contest if truth be told. We were too good at what we do; we picked our targets, put them down and moved on to the next. Like the first one I killed back in the cavern they all took a while to realize they were dead but in ten seconds flat we'd taken down all of the man-sized beasts, reducing them to a pile of bloody bodies on the sand. The big one was the last remaining. It glared at us, then astonished me again by pointing at Her Majesty and shouting the same word as before, as if it were a command he expected her to obey.

"Kunaja," he bellowed.

"Fuck off," Her Majesty bellowed back. He didn't like that much.

He put his head down and charged.

We took aim and fired.

It took all three of us, and most of the rounds we had in our mags, but he went down in the end, a bloody heap no more than two yards away. The light finally went out of his eyes as he died looking at Her Majesty with one hand outstretched towards her.

"Do you have a knife?" she said to me.

I handed her my blade without questioning, then we watched in horror as she went over to the beast and, with sawing motions that took far too long, cut off its cock at the base. She spat on the bloody thing, threw it into the sea and turned back to us.

"What does a girl have to do to get a fucking drink around here?"

***

Her Majesty has kept out of trouble since then, thank the Lord. She rarely leaves the yacht nowadays, a mixture of fear and the fact that she's as pregnant as I've ever seen anyone be. If she has the same thoughts as me she doesn't show it. The Sheikh is over the moon at the prospect of getting a son and heir and she does nothing to dissuade him from that. But the pregnancy bothers me, in the quiet reaches of the night.

I remember how long she was alone with the Minotaur. I remember how it tried so hard to keep her. I think about the herd of cattle I saw and wonder whether they'd actually been food…or had they been a harem?

But most of all, I think about that word the old one used. It bothered me so much I Googled it (the scholar that I am!)…and now wished I hadn't.

Kunaja, noun, pronounced *Ku-Na-Ja,* Mycenaean Greek, meaning 'wife'.

END

BONESAW RIDGE

Lucas Pederson

We're not gonna make it.

Jess slammed the deadbolt home and turned to the others. Every one of them was exhausted or hurt. Bleeding. Bruised. Battered.

"Door is half rotted," Zach said, nursing his left arm. Blood dripped from his fingertips to the dust-laden floor. He shook his head and paced. "We're so fucked."

Anna, the only one, except for Jess, unhurt, shot Zach a glare. "Settle down, man."

He chuckled humorlessly. "Settle down?" He stormed toward her, fist raised. "Settle *down*? Those things are going to bust right through that door any minute and kill us all, and you want me to fuckin' settle *down*?" He spun away and buried his fist into the nearest wall. Plaster shards clattered onto the floor. Dust puffed the air.

"This is why Ms. Sullivan didn't like you," Jess said. "Hell, I don't even like you. Like, I'd rather suck shit out of a two-year-old latrine than be around you."

"Hur-hur," Zach said and flipped her off. "You and Ms. Sullivan can go fall down a well, for all I care." He turned away. "Should've never signed up for this shit. I *knew* it was fucked."

"Jesus," Tim said. "Do you ever shut the hell up?" The big man, with a nasty, bloody claw mark across his barrelled chest stepped between Anna and Zach. "Take a damn breather, eh?"

"Breather? Those fuckin' things won't take a *breather*, man," Zach whined and paced the room. "We're so fucked."

Jess checked the magazine of her M4 carbine. It wasn't full by any means, but at least she had a few bullets to work with. Unless those things outnumbered their bullets. Then, as Zach kept repeating, they were fucked. She shoved the magazine home and glanced around. The house was old, probably a place for hunters to meet up and hang out after filling their tags. Maybe slam back more than a few beers as well.

If they still gathered at the house, though, there was no sign. And if so, they'd been neglecting dire repairs. Cracks cut through the walls and, in some spots, the plaster had broken free completely and lay scattered on the floor. A blanket of dust covered the rubble. The floorboards creaked and groaned while she walked around the first level.

Hunters or not, why anyone would want to build a two-storey house out in the middle of nowhere, especially on Bonesaw Ridge, was beyond her.

"We should see about boarding up the windows," Anna said.

Jess nodded, eyeing the nearest window, which was broken. When she moved closer to it, glass crunched under her boots.

"Sullivan lied to us, didn't she," Anna said. It was not a question.

"Looks that way. That shit shower of a woman is gonna get hers soon as we get back."

Anna snorted. "Shit shower, eh?"

"It's funny because it's true," Jess said and faced Anna. "Okay, get the guys gathered up, shoot Zach in the face with a horse tranquilizer or something, and let's work on these windows."

Anna gave a nod, half-turned, then glanced at Jess. "You think we'll make it?"

"If we turn this place into a goddamn fortress, yes. Pick them off one by one from the second-floor windows—"

Breaking glass ripped the words right out of her throat. Anna's eyes widened as hisses filled the lower level of the old house.

"Ah, hell," Zach shouted. "We're so fucked!"

"They're in," Jess whispered to Anna.

Chitters tapped upon Jess's eardrums. Heart whip-cracking against her ribs, she lifted the M4. There were live rounds in every gun, despite it being a training exercise. That's how Jess liked it. Everything needed to be as real as possible during training.

Anna backpedaled, joining Jess and lifted her own rifle.

A long hiss, like air escaping a tire, floated through the old house. Jess pressed a finger to her lips. Anna nodded. They sidestepped into the entryway where the rest of the team stood. Zach paced while Tim joined Jess and Anna.

Zach continued to pace. The floorboards creaked and groaned under his boots, driving spikes of rage through Jess. She rushed at him, fist raised. He noticed and stopped the infernal pacing.

Before he could open his mouth, she punched his chest. Not hard, but enough to let him know she wasn't fucking around. She pressed a finger to her lips. In a perfect world, Zach would actually listen to her.

Unfortunately, it was far from perfect and Zach spouted, "How do we know they hunt by sound?"

It crashed through the wall behind Zach in a storm of plaster dust and splinters of lathing.

Jess yanked Zach away and squeezed the trigger. Her M4 burst to life. A squeal rose from somewhere in amongst the dusty storm. She stopped shooting and backed away. If only she had one more magazine. Just one...

But she didn't. If she were to guess, she had roughly a dozen bullets left. If that.

Her team stood beside her, all of them at the ready. Even Zach. Her finger cradled the trigger. But—

"The shit?" Zach whispered. "Where'd it go?"

Jess fought the urge to backhand him. Zach was the best sniper she'd ever had on a team. But the guy was obnoxious as hell. Before, she could ignore him, but now it was to the point of murder if he didn't quit flapping his damn jaw every two seconds.

Once all the dust settled, she saw what Zach so eloquently pointed out. The creature wasn't anywhere to be seen. A couple chunks of plaster fell and clunked on the floor from the ragged hole it created. The house fell into the deepest silence Jess had ever known. One drowning in dark foreboding. An obsidian soup of nothing.

Jess made Zach and Tim stand guard at the doorway to the small dining area where Anna and she stood before the thing broke in. With Anna once more by her side, they moved toward the hole in the wall. Jess tried to control the quickening of her heart, but it was no use.

She fought small armies. Assassinated dictators and vile religious leaders. Her and her team took down more than a few growing regimes. But never in her life had she imagined coming up against a real monster. A creature from out of nowhere. Was it an alien? Some unnamable monstrosity from below the earth? A lab experiment gone horribly wrong? *What?*

Questions plagued her mind, and they shouldn't. They added to the fear building inside. They fed it. Kill them all. That's the singular thought which needed to replace all the questions. Kill them all and ask questions later. It's how it should be. How it had been...until coming face to face with real monsters.

The holes in the wall led into a larger room with furniture. Couch. Loveseat. Recliner. A living room. The creature wasn't in there either. Her boots crunched over chunks of plaster. She cringed at the noise, fearful of what it might attract.

Where the hell is it? Jess stopped walking, frowning at the living room. Her gaze drifted over the broken glass on the floor from one of the windows. Other than that, there was no sign of the creature.

The rest of her team joined her in the living room. Tim slumped against a wall, looking far too pale.

64

"I think it went back out," Jess whispered. "We need to board up as many windows as we can."

Zach chuckled humorlessly. "Yeah, that'll work. C'mon, man. We're sitting ducks here."

"Where the hell are we supposed to go?" Jess asked, stepping closer to him. "This is the only form of protection we got right now."

"We have nowhere to go," Anna whispered. "This is it."

Zach opened his mouth, then closed it again. He sighed and turned away from Jess and Anna.

"If you want to live," Jess said. "Get to the second floor and pick 'em off when you see 'em."

He nodded and, remarkably, said nothing before finding the stairs.

Jess turned her attention to Tim, who rested against the wall, head lowered. Saliva stringed from his mouth to the floor. "You okay, Tim?"

The big man shook his head. "Uh, yeah. Just tired." When he lifted his head to look at her though, blood trickled from the corners of his eyes. He sagged a bit, legs quivering to hold him up.

Anna and Jess hurried to him before he collapsed.

"Just...tired," Tim muttered, head lolling. "S-sorry."

They helped him to the couch and laid him down.

"Rest," Jess said.

Her gaze drifted to her comrade's chest where his shredded shirt revealed just enough of the man's skin. The claw mark across his chest continued to bleed. Curiously, the skin around the scratches was black.

Tim mumbled something about being too tired before his eyes slipped shut and he fell asleep.

Jess and Anna backed away from him.

"I've seen him get shot in the leg and shoulder and still push on," Anna said. "That scratch shouldn't do this to him."

Jess nodded, thinking about her sister, Dani. They were seventeen and, out of nowhere one day while swimming, Dani broke out in strange, red blotches which turned black in a matter of hours. Jess' baby sister died a week later after the blotches appeared. To this day, she wasn't exactly sure what killed Dani. Sometimes, there wasn't an answer. Sometimes, people just died for no reason at all. But no reason at all left loved ones without closure. Jess missed her…everyday.

She watched Tim for a moment while he snored away on the couch. A nearly seven-foot tall, two-hundred-eighty-pound man who never rested until Jess said so. Despite the superficial wounds, the guy was out. It didn't make sense to her. Nor to Anna, judging by the woman's furrowed eyebrows.

"So," Zach said, stepping beside Jess. "How are we supposed to board up the windows if we don't have boards, or nails?" He frowned at Tim. "What's wrong with Timmy?"

She sighed. "Stack furniture, whatever we can find. Anything to slow the bastards down. And I don't know. And, what the hell are you doing down here?"

He shrugged. "Figured I'd help out a bit before setting up."

They worked as quickly as possible stacking and piling anything and everything in front of as many windows as they could. Which amounted to only three. There just wasn't much to work with. The loveseat blocked the broken window. Kitchen table and chairs partially covered another, while the recliner blocked only about half of the final window.

"Christ," Zach said, glancing at the windows. "We're so fucked."

"Hey," Jess said, keeping her voice low. "It's not over until it's over. Got me? Now get upstairs and keep watch."

Zach rolled his eyes, grabbed his rifle, and tromped up the stairs.

"I kinda wish one of the steps would've broke under him," Anna whispered.

Jess snorted. "We can't get that lucky. Let's keep watch down here too and hope those things have moved on."

Anna took the window with the recliner, facing west while Jess settled on the opposite side where the creature broke in.

She peered through small gaps in the pile. Lush and green, the woods of Bonesaw Ridge stood in complete silence. Not even an errant breeze rustled the leaves or brush. Like being trapped in the eye of a hurricane. Jess's heart thudded heavily. Sweat beaded her forehead. No place should be so quiet. So…dead still. It was all wrong. All of it.

A seasoned a team of mercenaries, they had been in some deep, scary hellholes before, but never like this. Monsters weren't supposed to exist for shitsake. Did Ms. Sullivan know about the creatures? It was her idea to have them train in the Bonesaw Ridge woods, after all. If so, why? They were her best team. Why would Sullivan send them out to die? If Jess and the team died, the woman would have to find a new, and probably less elite group to do her bidding. Highly paid bidding, but still…

None of it made any sense.

Jess moved to a different gap in the pile, barely registering the crackling sounds behind her. Probably just Anna cracking her knuckles, or something. Anna had a bad habit of doing that. Jess focused on the all the listless green outside. So green, she could smell it. A strong, leafy aroma which practically clogged the nostrils like a thick mucus.

There was another smell too. Something more…carnal. The metallic, minerally scent of blood.

A frown creased her face. Why did she smell blood? Jess, stomach churning, turned around. Tim's stomach bulged toward the ceiling like a pregnant person. His face had split down the middle and all that blood soaked into the couch.

For a few seconds, Jess couldn't find the strength to breathe. Finally, she whooped in a breath and blew it out in a mild torrent.

Tim's bulging stomach stretched farther, moving toward the ceiling. All the while, the swollen mass bulged and contracted. Something was moving inside. Something pressing and shifting against the membrane of skin.

"Oh, shit…" Anna whispered.

She stood in front of her window, eyes wide, staring at Tim's distended stomach. The bulge protruded a good three feet from Tim's body, thick sloshing noises issuing from the stomach.

Jess opened her mouth to tell Anna to shoot the bulge when something pointy burst out the side, slashing upward and splitting the already horribly stretched skin. Yellow fluid and blood spilled forth in a grotesque flood.

What tore out of Tim defied everything Jess believed in.

The thing perched on Tim's body, oddly humanlike hands ripping organs out and shoving them into a heavily toothed maw. Every now and then, that maw would snap out like a goblin shark to grab a dangling section of intestine. The arms were attached to its narrow chest. Other than those, nothing about the creature was human.

It mewled contentedly while it feasted on Tim's body. A long tail whipped and lashed at the air behind it. At its end was a curved, black barb. The pointy thing that cut through the skin, Jess realized. The rest of its body was something between a spider and crab. It appeared to have a shell to it. Gray in color. Sharp spines jutted irregularly all over its body. Its oblong head boasted several black eyes.

Jess tried more than once to stow the terror and blast the creature. Tried, and failed. And it was only a baby. The others were much larger.

It all began to sink in then. Tim was scratched across the chest. The contact infected the man with…what? An egg? Larvae of some description? Even though none of it made sense, she needed to accept that, in a way, it did make sense. She was no scientist, but what other explanation was there?

Monsters were real and one of them was feasting on the remains of the best point-man she'd ever known. A man that could crush a skull and hug you seconds later. A man who really didn't have to be a mercenary but chose to anyway.

Anna fired first.

Her rounds struck the creature directly in the head. It squealed, higher in pitch than the other one, and scrambled off Tim. It clattered on the floor. Fell. Its humanlike arms and hands groped, trying to pull it toward the ragged hole in the wall.

Whatever held Jess in sway broke. She stormed toward it. Shoved the muzzle of her M4 against its ugly head and pulled the trigger.

Dark blood splattered the air.

It jittered, made a gurgling sound, then fell silent. Its eight legs curled up toward its narrow body, joints popping. Its maw extended, it snapped at the air a couple of times before falling limp on the floor.

Jess waited several seconds, but the thing didn't move. She even kicked it to be sure. Nothing.

"What…" Anna managed as she shuffled toward Jess. "What's going on?"

Jess stepped over the creature and caught Anna before she lost her balance. The woman sagged against Jess for a moment, then straightened.

"Sorry."

"No need to be sorry," Jess said. Her heart skipped a beat remembering Zach had been scratched too. "We need to check on Zach."

Anna blinked. "Why?"

"Tim got wounded by one of those things," she explained. "So did Zach."

"You think that's the reason for that thing?" Anna asked.

"I don't know. C'mon."

Jess hurried up the stairs to the second floor, Anna following close behind. They found Zach in the northern most room of the house. He was laid on the floor, staring out the scope of his sniper rifle.

Jess released a long sigh of relief. "Hey. You see anything out there?"

Zach didn't move. Nor did he answer her.

Anna tapped Jess's arm and pointed at the side of Zach's face. A dark blotch grew on his visible cheek.

"Shit," Jess said.

"If we kill him now, will it stop the thing from growing?" Anna asked.

All Jess could do was shake her head.

Muffled crackling sounds issued from Zach. His back bowed upward.

"Shoot the bulge," Jess said watching the structure of Zach's back change as the thing inside severed his spine.

Anna positioned herself opposite Jess, nodding.

Jess pointed her M4 at the emerging bulge. "Fire!"

They blasted Zach's back with bullets. Jess stopped when her magazine was empty. The bulge shuddered, swayed, then drooped.

"I'm out," Jess said, ejecting the magazine.

"Zach has a mag it looks like," Anna said.

Well, hell, the woman was right. Jess took Zach's magazine and shoved it home into her M4. He may have been a sniper, but that didn't stop him carrying a carbine like everyone else. It was the one time she forgave him for breaking the rules and bringing more than one mag to a training exercise.

"How many rounds do you have?" Jess asked Anna.

"Fifty. Or around there. I think."

Jess nodded, although she assumed the woman was off a bit. She had to be close to empty considering how much she used the weapon. She pulled Zach's sniper rifle way from him and said, "Grab Tim's mag and get back up here."

Anna hesitated a second or two before hurrying back down the stairs.

From the vantage point, Jess still didn't see anything that would…

Something gray scrambled behind a thicket. She pointed the sniper rifle in the direction and looked through the scope. It didn't take long to spot the creature. Nor did it take much effort to see the others crouched down and hiding behind the veil of green. They were surrounding the house. Quietly assembling and advancing through the woods.

"Fuck," she whispered, watching more than six moving through the thick brush.

"Okay," Anna said behind her. "Got it."

"They're advancing," Jess said, still looking through the scope. "Sixty yards out."

"How many?" Anna asked.

"I don't know. I see six. Might be more. No telling how many are surrounding us."

Anna paused. Her breathing grew shallow, her voice barely a whisper. "Surrounding us?"

"More than likely," Jess said.

"So, what are we going to do?"

The monsters never stopped advancing.

Jess sighed. "I might be able to take out all six on this side right now."

Anna didn't even hesitate. "Then do it."

Jess lowered to the floor, aimed at the far-right creature, and fired. It stopped moving instantly, sections of its carapace flying in all directions. She swung the gun to the next in line and picked that one off as well, bits and pieces scattering. Before long, all six were dead. Jess stood, grabbed the rest of Zach's rifle ammo, and rushed across the hall to the opposite side of the house. Mostly south. Maybe southwest. There she spotted another group sneaking through the green brush. Over a dozen, she noted. Maybe more.

It's like they knew where Zach was looking. And yet, Zach was impregnated by them. Maybe they messed with his mind. Could they do that?

Jess stopped at ten, running out of ammo.

She dropped the sniper rifle. "They'll be coming through the lower level. I'll take that position."

"No," Anna said. "I'll do it."

Jess frowned. "It'll be safer up here."

Anna paused. She appeared to think about it for a moment or two then shook her head. "I have more ammo than you."

Jess sighed. The last thing she wanted was to have Anna devoured by those things. So, she said, "Stay on the second level with me then. We'll take 'em out as they come up the stairs. Aim for the heads."

Jess and Anna positioned themselves on either side of the second-floor hall.

Clattering from downstairs. A few heavy thumps. The crash of breaking glass. There was no question about it, they were inside.

Jess pressed a shoulder against the staircase wall opposite Anna, risked a glance down the stairs. A series of chitters drifted up the steps reaching her ears, followed by loud hisses. Besides the noises, nothing came up the stairs. She moved back and looked at Anna.

The woman's face, slick and gleaming with sweat, gaped back at Jess. Her eyes were so wide Jess almost wanted to cup her hands under the woman's eyes just in case they popped out of their sockets. The terror baked off Anna and Jess couldn't really do much to calm her. It'd give away their position.

The only thing she could do was gently pat the air with her hand. A gesture she hoped told Anna to calm down. The woman must have understood because she nodded. Ann drew in a breath, blew it out slowly. Nodded again. Her gaping expression closed a bit and she readied herself against the wall.

Jess smiled. Anna got scared a lot, but she also had a great deal of steel in her. All it took was for her to draw that steel up and block out the fear. Over the years, Jess witnessed that very thing happen a lot and it never ceased to put a smile on her face.

A very loud hiss blew up the stairs, yanking Jess's attention away from Anna. She crouched, finger sliding over the trigger of her M4.

This is our last stand, she thought. Her jaw clenched. *This is it. Kill or be killed.*

Something clacked. The steps groaned. Closer and closer.

Jess leaned back, ready to swing around the side of the wall. Tension, like dozens of crisscrossing steel cables, slowly tightened around her.

Clack. Groan. Very close now.

Jess shot a glance at Anna, who nodded in reply.

They swung around their walls to face the creature on the stairs. It flinched, clattered backward on its spiny legs.

It didn't have time for anything else.

Jess and Anna opened fire. Bits and pieces of its head blew away. Black blood sprayed the walls on either side of the staircase. The creature let out a thin whine and tumbled backward down the steps to the first floor.

Jess watched its legs twitch, then ducked back behind the wall. Anna followed suit.

The noises downstairs intensified.

Anna shook her head. "We're not gonna make it."

She echoed Jess' thought from the very beginning, and it jarred her a bit. Maybe it was true. Maybe they were doomed from the start. That didn't mean giving up, and that's what Anna appeared to be doing.

"We fight," Jess whispered. "'Til the end. We fight."

Anna straightened, managed a weak smile. "We fight."

A few more clacks scrambled up the stairs.

They swung out and turned the monster's head to pulp. It flipped backward, joining its likewise dead kin. A couple more met the same fate.

"I'm about out," Anna whispered, holding her M4 up a bit.

Jess tossed her what was left in her old mag.

Glass shattered somewhere down the hall.

Anna's eyes widened.

Jess stood up straight. More clacks and chitters made their way up the staircase.

She focused on Anna. "Don't forget we have sidearms. Get the thing on the stairs. I'll take out whatever broke—"

The creature scrambled out of a room at the far end of the hall, shrieked and scuttled toward Jess and Anna.

Jess sprang forward and shot at the creature's head. It shifted the slightest bit, bullet going wild.

"Shit."

It surged forward on its spidery-crablike legs.

She sighted the monster in once more and let loose. The problem with the creatures was their shell. It took a few rounds to actually weaken and break through it. Half its head disintegrated, and it crashed to the floor.

Jess spun around and froze. A creature held Anna in its human like hands. Her head lolled from side to side.

Battle fog drifted over Jess. She roared, startling the monster. It lowered Anna and Jess blew a good portion of its head off. She managed to grab Anna before it tumbled down the stairs. More crowded around the bottom, a tide of chitin swelling upward.

Anna moaned and patted her shoulder where the clothing had been split and blood welled from a deep scratch. She shook her head at Jess.

"You'll be okay," Jess said, dragging Anna down the hall and over the spiny corpse of a creature. She took Anna not into the last room, but second to last on the opposite side of the hall. Barren and blanketed with dust, Jess laid Anna on her back in there.

"Get out," Anna said before coughing up a spattering of blood. "Just...run."

"No," Jess said. "We fight, remember?"

Anna coughed up more blood, chuckling. "Bullshit. Something is growing inside me. I feel it. Hurts like hell. You can't kill them all, Jess. You don't have enough ammo."

Jess cupped Anna's cheek. "I'm not leaving you."

"You fucking better," Anna said. "You...you're the only one who can get someone out here to napalm the place—ah, shit, I feel it growing, Jess. It fucking hurts!"

"I can't," Jess said, hating how the tears welled in her eyes.

Anna, despite her agony, managed a smile. "You can. Now go."

"I—"

"*Go!*" Anna shouted.

Jess kissed the woman's forehead. "Thank you for all of it. Thank you for being my best friend."

Anna's smile lengthened. "I always loved you, Jess."

Clacking and hissing sounded from the hallway.

Anna sighed. "Go."

Jess wiped tears from her cheeks, quickly snapping Anna a salute.

Anna, very weak, managed one back before her hand plopped to the floor in a plume of dust.

A loud hiss broke through everything.

Jess spun to find one of the creatures dominating the doorway. She didn't know how many rounds were in her magazine, nor cared. She unloaded on the monster.

It charged just as her mag ran dry, shoving her out the window.

For a split-second, she thought she was flying. Then...nothing.

***

Chirping sounds bounced off the walls of her skull.

Jess woke with a gasp lying on her back. The green canopy of barley filtered the dying light. Unlike before, the leaves rustled in

75

vagrant breezes. She had a moment or two to think it had all been some horrific nightmare, when something chittered nearby.

She forced her eyes shut and tried to relax her body.

The creature chuffed inches from her ear. Dirt dusted the side of her head.

Don't move. Let it think you're dead.

Sharp pain stabbed into her arm, but she refused to scream. Refused to let it win. So, she held it all in and waited. The thing was testing her. Seeing if she was alive or dead. Only problem would be was if it chose to eat her, regardless what it thought.

Then it sank its teeth into her shoulder.

Jess roared. Not entirely in pain, but hatred. She drew her sidearm from its holster, rolled to the side, and jammed the muzzle of the pistol against the creature's head. Its numerous black eyes blinked back at her, almost as if it was confused.

She pulled the trigger until the monster collapsed beside her.

Heart bashing itself against the walls of her chest, Jess stood, wincing. She sucked in a sharp breath through clenched teeth. Pain exploded all over, but none so bad as her right leg where a long shard of glass was stuck in her thigh. Chitters filled the space behind Jess. A long hiss joined in. The clicking of shelled legs working together came next.

With every step, agony shot through her. Still, she limped away from the house until the pain became too much. The chitters and hisses drew closer. Louder, too.

Jess stopped, her head lowered to the ground. A rough sigh filtered out of her. Images of her beloved sister Dani shuffled across her mind's eye. Images of their childhood. Swimming in the local lake. Camping. Fishing. Melting plastic dolls on Dad's grill then catching hell for it. So many memories in such a short amount of time.

She blinked and the images faded. A tear slipped down Jess' cheek. She switched the sidearm to her left hand, wiped away the tear. The hissing swelled behind her. So close now, she felt their sour breath beat against her back.

"We fight," she whispered, holding the M4 in her right hand.

Jess spun, the sidearm and M4 held high, one in each hand.

"We—"

Both guns went off before Jess' eyes relayed what they saw to her brain. By that time, it was too late.

The M4 sheared off a portion of Anna's head while the bullet expelled from her sidearm plunged into an eye. Anna's head snapped backward, blood spurting into the air.

Jess dropped the sidearm a fraction of a second later. The air fled from her lungs. Her mouth opened and closed like a beached fish. Her bowels cramped.

Anna's head lolled. She fell to her knees, body twitching.

Breaking out of her shock, Jess caught the woman before she hit the ground. She pulled Anna close, cradling her.

"No," Jess said over and over. "*No.*"

She rocked Anna's body. Rocked and rocked. Tears spilled down her face in hot streams. *Ah, gods,* Jess thought. *What did I do?*

But Anna was supposed to stay in the house. Anna was infected. Why was she outside? *How* was she outside?

Muffled crackling came from somewhere inside the dead woman. Ribs snapping; spine breaking. Something writhed in her stomach, nudging Jess. She gasped, but couldn't let Anna go, only vaguely aware of the creatures gathered around her. She refused to look at them. Refused to listen to the chitters and hisses.

They let Anna out of the house, Jess came to realize. A way to trick her into not running.

Didn't matter now.

Eventually, the pointy barb at the end of the newborn creature's tail shot out of Anna, stabbing Jess just below the sternum. She cried out, but still didn't let her friend go.

The monster slashed out of Anna and rose before Jess.

The others scuttled closer.

Jess stared at the creature's dripping maw and closed her eyes.

THE END

A MAN OF HIS WORD

Alister Hodge

A scream lacerated the air, destroying the early morning silence. Instantly awake, Vito sat bolt upright, his hand reaching for a blade. Cliffs to the east of the oasis were backlit in grey as the approaching dawn lightened the sky. He cocked his head to the side and listened, deep lines of concentration carved into his forehead. A breeze ruffled the branches of a date palm overhead, but aside from the snoring of soldiers nearby, there was nothing more.

A wild cat, maybe?

The arid wastes sometimes mutated sound in the emptiness of night, turning a simple birdcall into a demonic wail. Despite a year stationed in the fractious border province, Vito had yet to grow comfortable in the region. Sheathing his dagger, he climbed to his feet, muscles creaking in protest.

As a Centurion of the 12th Legion, Vito led by example. Like every soldier under his command, he'd slept under the stars fully dressed, with hob-nailed sandals on foot. In the field, he wore his lamellar armour like a second skin, ready to fight at a moment's notice. Vito scooped his helmet off the ground and shoved it on his head, chewing at the inside of a cheek. Something wasn't right, and after twenty years of fighting for the Empire, he'd learnt to trust his gut.

Spies for the legion had recently detected whispers of insurrection, of a desert camp led by a charismatic holy man who promised liberation from Rome's iron fist. Acting on the information,

Vito had led eighty men on a mission to stamp out the embers of uprising before it spread like wildfire.

Following a local guide named Pyroe, Vito's unit had trekked into the desert. The monotonous expanse of dunes, interspersed by sandstone valleys of blood-red stone, soon morphed into one. A haze had stretched from one horizon to the other for much of the trek, stealing the stars and blocking the sun's orb during day. Last night, the sky had finally cleared for a few hours, allowing Vito to gain a sense of his bearings from the constellations. The added information had done little to settle a growing sense of disquiet at the route of his guide.

He'd heard more than one soldier grumbling that the weather was a bad sign. Vito rarely gave the gods a second thought, nor did he believe in omens. He's seen too many soothsayers bribed for a fortuitous reading to put any weight in predictions. And the gods? Even if they *were* real, why would such powerful entities pay interest to the petty squabbling of humans? To a god, humans must be of less interest than a blowfly to an elephant. No, Vito trusted in the bite of his sword, the protection of his shield, and the bravery of his comrades. The 12th Legion was his family and life, and there was nothing else he needed.

Last night, Pyroe led them into a narrow valley bordered by sandstone cliffs to access a water source. Vito's tactical mind had loathed to take his men into such an environment, but with water bladders nearing empty, he'd little choice. True to the guide's word, they'd found a spring-fed lake of clear water, surrounded by grass and tall, date palms. A true desert oasis, small silver fish swam in the shallows while crocodiles occupied the deeper water, eyes breaching the surface to watch the human interlopers. The water had energised parched bodies, but the surrounding terrain filled Vito with unease as they camped. To warn of an ambush, he'd installed sentries on the cliffs and pickets about the camp, before gaining a few short hours of sleep.

The scream sounded again. Harsh, long and filled with despair, like a tortured soul wishing for death. Vito turned and searched the cliffs, realising it came from where he'd set one of the sentries. No-one slept through the second scream. Soldiers rose in the half-light like wraiths, quickly rolling sleep mats and readying themselves for action.

"Centurion?" An officer called Felix approached, brows knotted with concern. "The baggage handlers are gone."

Vito swore bitterly, now certain they sat in the teeth of a trap. The guide had seen to hiring the camels and men of their supply train. If they'd scarpered without pay, trouble was surely afoot.

"Get the men into a defensive formation, and bring that bastard, Pyroe, to me."

The officer nodded, shouting orders as he jogged off to find the guide. Vito picked up his shield and slipped the grip over his left forearm. Long and rectangular with a slight curve, it reached from shoulder to knee. From habit, he loosened his gladius sword in its scabbard, then paced to the edge of the oasis. Reaching his outer picket, he returned the soldiers' salute with a nod and squatted down beside them, staring out to the land beyond.

"The camel handlers have fled," said Vito. "Did you see anything?"

"No, sir. Nothing passed through our lines, they must have found a different path out of the gorge." The legionnaire grimaced and spat into the dirt. "So, if the locals have all fucked off, I take it we're about to be attacked." It wasn't voiced as a question. "I sent Marius to investigate that scream—"

A short, guttural cry sounded from above. Sky lined on the clifftop stood Marius with his hands bound, a robed figure at his back. With brutal efficiency, his captor ripped a knife across the legionnaire's throat. Arterial blood, dark in the early light, spurted in an arc. The robed man kicked a foot into Marius' back and suddenly the soldier was falling, a tangle of limbs in the air until he hit the ground with a crunch.

"Form up on me!" roared Vito. He needed to get out of the valley before their avenues of escape were sealed.

Legionnaires jogged from amongst the palms and formed a square with practiced efficiency, two lines deep at all margins, prepared for attack from any direction. At a tap on his shoulder, Vito stepped back from the foremost rank into the square's centre to find Felix holding their guide by the scruff of his neck. Pyroe rung his hands, a prickling of sweat across his forehead.

"Honoured Centurion, I am a servant of Rome. I've served you faithfully, have I not? Please do not hurt me."

Vito grit his teeth. He trusted the guide about as far as he could throw him. "If you've led us into an ambush, I'll bloody crucify you for such a betrayal."

"I have done as ordered. You hunt the rebels, and I have brought you to an arranged meeting to 'negotiate' with their leader," said Pyroe, words tumbling out. "I thought you'd jump at a chance to kill the man?"

"Not here I wouldn't, you fool." Vito backhanded him, taking small satisfaction as claret spurted from Pyroe's nose. "While we sit at the bottom of this gorge, the enemy holds the advantage of high ground."

"It was the only place they would meet, there was no choice," wailed the guide.

"Sir! We have company," shouted a soldier.

Vito clenched his fist, aching to beat Pyroe's face to a pulp, but instead turned to see who approached.

The robed figure who had slit Marius' neck now walked slowly from the southern end of the gorge. One of the legionnaires raised a javelin, an iron tipped pilum, ready to throw.

"Wait."

Although the enemy remained hidden, Vito thought it likely that a force lined the cliff just out of sight. If he wanted to extricate his unit intact, he had little choice but to humour the bastards. For now, at least.

The robed man paced forward, face buried in shadow until he slid off his hood. The first rays of morning streamed over the cliff top, bathing him in yellow light. Red and blue tattoos covered a shaved scalp and curled across his face and neck. A mixture of stylised pictures and illegible text, they seemed to writhe and move across his skin. The man stopped twenty paces away and stared at the legionnaires, lip curled with scorn. After a few moments, he undid a string at his neck and let the robe drop to the ground.

"By Mithras," muttered Vito.

The man was naked. The tattoos of face and neck continued unbroken across his entire body, genitals included. Lines of age carved deep into the man's face, while the skin of his belly hung loose, telling of an obese body reduced to emaciation. Barefoot, he stepped away from the robe and stood with a knife clenched in one hand, a clay gourd in the other.

"Pyroe, who is he?"

The guide peered over a legionnaire's shoulder. His pupils dilated, breath coming a little quicker.

"He's the Bārû."

"The what? Speak Latin, you idiot."

"The Bārû is a powerful seer who can communicate with the gods and demand their presence. It is an honour to even lick the dust from his feet!"

"Fuck that," grated Vito. "Tell him I want the location of the rebel force, and that they're to surrender or be crucified. The province will learn Rome doesn't tolerate rebellion."

Pyroe's face blanched, but he did as ordered, stammering out words in the local dialect. The Bārû ignored the guide, choosing to address Vito directly instead. The seer had a deep voice that carried, bouncing off the gorge walls in a rumbling echo.

"What's he saying? Translate," ordered the Centurion.

"The Romans are unwelcome invaders to our land," started Pyroe, nervously licking his lips, eyes flicking between the two leaders. "You will pay the ultimate price for your trespass. Rome's lifeblood will cleanse the land, freeing our people of Latin perversions to follow the religion and practices of our culture."

The seer began to pour liquid from the gourd as he spoke, creating a circle about himself. A murmur of disquiet filtered through the legionnaires as a rancid, coppery smell reached their noses.

"Is that blood?" asked Vito, his nose wrinkling.

Within the circle, the Bārû created a series of geometric patterns before tipping the last of the blood onto his chest, creating a stripe of crimson from neck to penis, where it dripped to the hungry sand. Finished, he flung the gourd aside.

"To rid us of this Roman pestilence, I call on a demon of the Underworld to rise!" Veins bulged at his temple, spittle flying as he screamed. "Through my sacrifice, I command the Galla demon of Kur to rise from the shadows and fight at our side!"

The seer plunged his knife deep into his belly. With short tugging motions, he ripped the blade upwards, severing the muscles of his abdominal wall until he reached his ribs.

Vito stared, eyes fixed to the scene in fascinated horror.

How is he still standing?

The Bārû's blade continued onwards, spreading the skin over his sternum and laying the white bone open to the morning sun. As the first loops of intestine spilled to the sand, the seer finally collapsed to his knees. With a last heaving gasp, he gripped the edges of his abdominal wound and spread them wide.

"Enter!" The last translated command was barely a whisper as the Bārû shuddered with agony.

Suddenly, the ancient's body jerked upwards. Hands spread high as if hung by invisible hooks, the seer's toes barely touched the ground.

Pyroe began to laugh manically. "It has worked. Galla comes!"

Vito spun the guide about. "What the hell's happening?"

"The Bārû's summoned a demon to slay all Romans!" said Pyroe. "No blade from this world can kill it. When the Galla takes your worthless lives with its sacred axe, your souls will be sucked to the underworld of Kur for eternity!"

Vito longed to kill the guide where he stood, but a promise was a promise. Pyroe's death would be a slow one. "I'm tired of this man's yammering," spat the Centurion. "Tie him up."

Felix ripped the guide's hands behind his back and bound them with a length of cord before shoving him to the middle of the square. New movement drew Vito's eye. Red light began to glow along the length of the seer's wound as the abdomen bulged. Something was in the man's gut, causing the skin to undulate like a bag of eels. A clawed hand emerged, then a head.

By Mithras, it's real.

The wound stretched impossibly wide as a grey-skinned, humanoid creature lunged through. Streaked with mucous, shit and blood, it dragged a huge axe out of the abdominal portal before rising to its feet. Vito's gut clenched. He'd stood his ground in countless battles over the decades, stared death in the eye and spat at fate, and yet, he'd never seen anything like this. Standing over nine feet tall, the Galla looked like granite brought to life. Dark grey, its skin was glistening with mucous. Black fangs filled a cavernous mouth below dead, psychopathic eyes. Aside from two nasal slits that flared with every breath, its face was almost flat.

Vito's eyes were drawn to the Galla's axe. The blade was crafted from a metal he'd never seen. Olive in colour, it emitted a faint glow as shades of green rippled across its surface. The demon gave the axe a lazy swing, and at the movement, a keening note of hunger emanated from the blade.

The seer collapsed to his knees, face pale and dripping with sweat. He drew a shuddering breath and coughed scarlet. With a shaking hand, he pointed at the Roman soldiers.

"Kill them all."

The last of his energy expended, the ancient man slumped to the ground, dead. The Galla ignored the demise of its summoner and stalked toward Vito's men with a low snarl. The front line of the square contracted, some of the men taking a half step back. The Centurion could feel hesitation amongst his soldiers.

"Hold your ground!" snarled Vito. "It's just a tall prick with an axe. Hack the legs, and he won't look high and mighty for long."

A hollow whistle of fletching cut the air, followed by a garbled scream. Vito turned to see a legionnaire scrabbling at his throat, an arrow with black feathers jutting from his neck.

Fuck.

An upward glance identified rebels lining the eastern rim of the gorge. The single projectile had been a sighting arrow to help the bowmen judge distance. Holding recurved bows, light glinted off spiked arrow heads as they drew as one. Vito swallowed as the bowmen loosed a volley, the steel-tipped shafts arcing towards them in a swarm of whispering death.

"Form Testudo!" shouted Vito.

With practiced economy of movement, the square contracted into a tight block of soldiers. Those on the outer edges overlapped shields to make an impenetrable wall, while soldiers in the centre of the formation raised their shields overhead. Like a tortoise tucked into its shell, the men were now protected as the arrows drove home, stabbing into the shields with a dull *thunk!* Created by gluing three layers of wood together, the long scutum shields were then covered in canvas and leather. Although incredibly strong for their weight, they weren't invincible. Vito's scutum shuddered as it was struck, an arrowhead punching through a finger's width, narrowly missing his grip.

He looked at the advancing demon, now just twenty paces distant. The testudo might protect against arrow fire, but it would be useless against the encroaching beast. They had to try and take him out before he reached the periphery of the shield wall. Vito lowered his shield and grasped a pilum javelin. Standing to full height, he drew his arm back and launched the javelin with all his strength, expecting an arrow to stab into his body at any second. The pilum flew true, plunging deep into the Galla's stomach.

Vito's brief satisfaction faltered as the demon barely broke stride. The Galla wrenched the javelin from its flesh, dropping it with contempt. Unbelievably, the abdominal wound sealed within a heartbeat, leaving its slimy skin unmarked. The demon batted away a second javelin with the haft of his axe and roared, black spittle flying. It lunged forward and smashed into the shield wall, using its shoulder as a battering ram. Two legionnaires were thrown off their feet and the Galla swept his axe in a devastating arc to widen the gap. The blade sliced through the helmet of the nearest soldier like parchment, plunging onward to take off the top of his skull like a soft-boiled egg. Brains splattered across the face of the next soldier as the corpse fell, joints unhinging as one.

The deadly hail of arrows continued. Tucked behind the shield wall, their ability to attack was hampered, and yet without it, they'd be decimated by the archers. Vito looked back to the oasis and thicket of date palms surrounding the water. He needed to get his men where the branches of the trees would provide cover and allow him to retaliate.

"To the tree line, retreat in formation!"

Needing little encouragement, his soldiers obeyed at speed. Swearing at the difficult manoeuvre, they jostled and bumped against each other in the press. Under the shields, it was difficult to appreciate the terrain and more than one soldier stumbled, nearly falling beneath the feet of their comrades.

The Galla easily kept pace, chopping at the shields and men before him. With every strike into human flesh, the axe blade emitted a metallic scream, sucking the soul of its victim into the metal with an odd shimmer of light. It didn't matter where the blade fell. If it drew blood, the soldier fell, the body left behind a bloody husk as its life-force was sucked to the Underworld.

Finally, they reached shade beneath the first stand of palms, sand giving way to desiccated grass. Roman corpses were scattered in their wake, a grim line of bloody destruction stretching from the desert sand to the oasis. Vito waited until they were under a greater density of trees before giving the order to break formation.

At his command, the testudo disintegrated, soldiers spreading apart into a staggered line, forming up three rows deep. Vito grimaced as he saw less than two-thirds of his force remained.

"Pilums!"

The first line raised their javelins. Created with a design unique to the Roman legions, the pilum consisted of a wooden shaft, tipped by a long spike of soft iron that could bend on impact. Once bent, it rendered the weapon useless to the enemy, stopping it from being thrown back at their own troops. The Galla staggered, forced back two steps as it was impaled by ten javelins in the space of a few seconds. Roaring with anger, it stopped to rip out the shafts. Two punched through his abdomen, front to back, forcing the demon to draw the javelins through his body entirely.

"Flank him!"

Taking the opportunity while the creature was distracted, Vito led the right side of the first line, curling around to attack the demon from behind. Like a set of horns, the left flank followed suit, creating a ring of sharpened steel about the Galla.

Vito held his gladius sword. A short, double-edged weapon with a viciously tapered point, it was designed for close combat. He'd carried this particular blade for over twelve years, and it was with the weapon in hand that he felt whole. Vito was a cog in the Roman military machine. He knew it, revelled in the power and professionalism of the soldiers he commanded. They may have been ambushed, but the enemy would pay with blood and lives. Adrenaline surged as he charged, all sense of fear forgotten as his training took over.

Seeing their comrades about to complete the encirclement, those in front of the demon attacked with renewed ferocity, voices hoarse. The monster towered over the legionnaires, their heads barely reaching the demon's waist. The Galla swept his axe in a low arc, severing the legs of two men below the knees. Hot blood spurted from severed arteries as they tumbled to the ground, their cries of agony abruptly cut off as the axe consumed their souls in a blink of light. A back swing took out another three soldiers, continuing the slaughter.

"No!"

Vito chopped his sword blade into one of the Galla's achilles, the tendon giving way with the sound of snapping wood. The demon staggered to a knee, bringing the beast's torso within reach. Vito took the opportunity before the wound healed and drove the point of his blade up into its back. A second heave against the pommel shoved the blade to its hilt, the point punching out above the Galla's collar bone.

The demon roared, black blood spattering its chest as it whipped a hand behind. Its fingers latched onto Vito's arm and wrenched him off his feet. With a grunt, the Galla threw him like a toy. Vito cartwheeled through the air, trees and ground a blur until he landed in the shallows of the lake with a mighty splash. Small fish darted away as a cloud of silt spread in the water.

The Centurion shook his head, trying to clear stars from his vision. He'd hit hard. A stabbing pain radiated from his lower back, shooting down his left thigh like lightning. He forced himself to stand, teeth grinding as a sprained ankle threatened to topple him once again. A swirl of water made him glance over his shoulder, just in time to see a Nile crocodile submerge. If he'd seen one of the bastard reptiles, there were bound to be others.

Turning back to his main threat, Vito tried to ignore the toothed monsters closing in from behind. With legionnaires trailing like dogs behind a bull, the demon stomped forward, closing in on Vito to finish the job. The Centurion had lost his shield in the fall, and as he slapped a hand to the scabbard at his waist, realised his sword was still buried in the beast's chest. He needed a weapon, *fast*.

"Someone throw me a sword so I can finish this whoreson!"

"Vito, catch!" Felix threw his sword overarm to land in the water next to his commander.

The Centurion squatted into the calf-deep water and took the weapon's grip, just as the Galla splashed into the edge of the spring. The demon charged with axe held over its head, kicking huge founts of water with every step. Vito forced himself to wait, muscles taut as a line of drawn copper. As the Galla brought his axe down, Vito dived forward with blade held to the side, aiming for the space between the demon's legs. The sword carved a deep line into the beast's inner thigh, hoping to slice a femoral artery.

On any other creature, it would have been a mortal wound, but within two squirts of tar-like blood, the wound sealed. Vito swore as he surfaced to find the Galla unharmed once again. There was only so long before he suffered an axe blow and followed his men to hell.

"Sir, you need to take his axe!" shouted Felix.

Vito grit his teeth at the interruption from the officer, before suddenly understanding what Felix meant. The local guide had said no weapon from *this world* could kill the demon, but the Galla had brought the axe with it through the portal from a very different land. The freakish, singing blade was from the Mesopotamian Underworld of Kur. Vito flashed a hard grin at his officer.

You bloody champion.

The Galla regained its balance and turned to face him again. Vito gripped the new sword, knuckles white. He needed to chop at the demon's arm. If he could cut the flexor tendons at the wrist, the beast would lose hold of the axe. Then he would have a chance. But with a short-sword designed for stabbing vital organs, it was going to be a tall order.

From his peripheral vision, he saw two humps of water surging towards the Galla's legs. The crocodile he'd seen slip beneath the water was a baby compared to these leviathans. At least sixteen feet in length, the first beast's head was longer than Vito's leg. Its jaws clamped about one of the Galla's ankles with the irresistible power of a cave-in. The demon looked down, lips withdrawn in disgust. It howled and chopped down with the axe into the reptile's back.

As the first crocodile's soul was stripped by the blade, a second beast latched onto the Galla's other leg. Huge teeth pierced the lower leg as the crocodile spun into a death roll. The power generated by the beast's movement tore off the demon's leg at the knee, dragging it into the turbid water.

It was now or never.

Vito charged through the water toward the Galla, chopping down at the hand holding the axe. His first blow cut part way through the wrist, revealing bone streaked with black blood. Before it had a chance to knit back together, Vito cut down with all his strength. This time, the gladius severed the limb, hand and axe splashing into the water. The demon lunged at him with its other hand, baring spiked teeth as it growled. Claws missed Vito's face by a hair's breadth, and then the crocodile dragged the demon out of reach with another vicious tug.

The Centurion dived beneath the water, searching frantically for the axe haft. Finally, his fingers closed about the wooden handle and he forced himself to stand. The bastard weapon had been designed for an immortal, not the puny musculature of a human. It took every fibre of his being to lift the unbelievable weight. Veins bulging with effort, Vito roared as he swung the axe in an ungainly arc over his head at the Galla. The blade emitted a high-pitched scream as it sliced into the angle between neck and shoulder, biting deep.

Black blood spurted from the wound as the axe head glowed. The weapon thrummed, rippling with green as it sucked the demon's lifeforce into the blade. The Galla fell limp, splashing facedown into the water. At the commotion, other crocodiles surfaced nearby, watching Vito and the corpse with dead-eyed hunger. Keeping an eye on the closest croc, Vito reclaimed his sword from the demon's back. It was time to reach dry ground.

Felix awaited him on the bank. "Another force approaches. The archers have come to support the beast, but this time they carry shield and sword."

Vito rolled his shoulders, a sour look on his face at the pain in his back. "Fucking idiots, the battle's over. Don't those pricks realise we just slaughtered their god?"

Felix shrugged. "All I know is the killing's not done for the day. What are your orders?"

"Form three ranks, and take prisoners if possible," growled Vito. "I made Pyroe a promise I intend to keep."

***

Vito stood back and observed his soldiers' work with satisfaction. It had taken less than twenty minutes to end the battle. Against veteran legionnaires, the rebels had been outclassed and quickly overpowered. The next part, however, had taken a little longer. After cutting two trunks and sawing the wood into beams, the legionnaires had hammered cross bars upon a number of the palms.

Only a handful of the enemy had the misfortune to survive the fight. Fifteen rebels now hung from the simple crucifixes, nails hammered through wrists and feet to hold them aloft. Most had stopped screaming, the weight of their own bodies slowly suffocating them in the unforgiving desert heat. There was not an inch of sympathy in the Centurion's body as he observed the horror enacted at his order. Vito's mind had long since grown dull to the suffering of others. To him, the exercise was nothing more than a tactic of war.

He turned to the last victim. Vito stared at Pyroe, the guide who had led them into the trap. Three soldiers held him against a palm trunk, ready to nail him in place. Sweat matted Pyroe's hair, his eyes wide, pupils dilated with terror.

"Centurion, this is a mistake," he panted. "I only serve the Empire."

"Really?" said Vito, an eyebrow raised. He waved a hand at the crucified enemy about them. "Do you call leading a century of Rome's soldiers into an ambush, *serving the Empire?*" Vito nodded at a soldier holding a mallet and nails, signalling for him to approach.

Pyroe watched the man, eyes fixed on the iron nails in his grip, each a handspan in length. "How will you escape the desert without my help? You will be lost, wandering the dunes until your men die of thirst."

Vito smirked. "I'm not that dumb, you idiot." He pointed upwards. "I'll use the map up there. I can read the stars, same as any boy from the country."

Pyroe blanched.

"That's right," nodded Vito. "I watched you lead us in circles for three days, until finally bringing us to this oasis when our water stores ran dry. I reckon we're less than a day and half from the main camp."

The soldier placed the tip of a nail against the guide's wrist, before looking back at the Centurion for final confirmation.

Vito nodded for him to continue. "Pin the bastard."

End

BLACK ICE

R.F. Blackstone

De Souza moaned, rubbing at his head. The man looked around, his eyes trying to focus. All around him he could hear the rest of the team groaning as they too slowly regained consciousness.

"Who's dead? Who's hurt? Who's alive?" he asked.

It took a few seconds for the rest of the team to answer, but slowly each one sounded off. Nero grunted then raised his hand. Monette winced as he put his dislocated shoulder back in place with a loud pop which caused the rest of the men to wince as he slammed his shoulder into the ground. Axel waved happily at the groups' leader, while Fischer and Wagner maintained their characteristic silence. The two men sat staring at the rest of the team, unblinking, forever guarding their brothers in arms.

"Where the flying fuck are we?" Nero asked as he stood and stretched, his vertebrae popping and cracking from the effort.

De Souza rubbed his face, his rough knuckles helping to relax his eyes and remove the chunks of dried gunk from them. Slowly, he too stood and stretched. The sensation of his muscles relaxing and his bones cracking made him feel at ease, if only slightly. He took a deep breath, then froze.

The air was thick with steam. His own breath as well as the rest of the team's. De Souza frowned. He hadn't noticed the cold at first. But the sensation of his bones aching and his teeth chattering soon filled him with a sense of dread.

Fuck! He thought. Turning he saw the spinning vortex that had deposited them slowly shrink until it vanished without a sound. The mixture of bright, almost fluorescent colours stung the man's eyes and a part of him was grateful they had been given Valium before the trip. De Souza raised an eyebrow. *So much for a quick exit,* he thought before looking at his men.

Monette picked up his Heckler & Koch G36C automatic rifle and inspected it, his forehead crinkling as his fingers ran over the weapon. There wasn't much he took pride in, but his weapons and skill at taking lives were top of the list. "Feels like a frozen cunt," he mumbled before spinning in place, his right eye pressed to the scope, scanning everyone and everything.

"I'd say it's Hel," Axel countered with a knowing smile.

Wagner shook his head before adding, "Your pagan bullshit isn't going to help here."

"And your kiddy-fiddlers will?" Axel said with a snort. "Or should we go with the Nationalists again?"

The others laughed, and De Souza couldn't help but join in. They were the best men he knew and this iteration of the Filthy Animals— his crew—was making him cash hand over fist. It wasn't just for him. They were all equal partners in the venture, and each got their fair share of the profits. Which was fine for all of them. The system worked, but just as with every job De Souza wondered, *Is this the one that fucks us all in the ass?*

"Boss?" Nero's voice interrupted the man's thoughts. "You okay, Boss?"

De Souza nodded, looked around and frowned. The file they had given him had no description of the location. All they gave him were the targets' names and co-ordinates. But whatever he was expecting in regard to the location, this was not it.

Coming from all sides, the men listened to the creaking and cracking of what could only be ice. Each loud groan from under the men made them tense up. "Lights on. Now!" De Souza ordered.

Flashlights flickered to life. Each of the Filthy Animals' shoulder-mounted lights cast small but powerful spotlights, but all they illuminated was darkness.

Emptiness.

Nothingness.

"This isn't right, mate," Monette said as he fumbled for a cigarette. From out of a heavy-duty vest pocket, he pulled forth an ancient-looking pack. His eyes were wild as he clamped his teeth down on the closest one to the pack's opening.

"Easy, Money," Nero said as he slowly turned in place. It was obvious the second-in-command was thrown off by the lack of... well...*anything*. "What you think, Boss?"

De Souza's eyes were focused on a shard of light twinkling next to him. His pale blue eyes focused hard on the peculiar reflection. A small smile crept across his face and he turned to his men. "It's black ice," he said, and his voice plunged the area into a deathly quiet.

"What the fuck is that?" Fischer asked, his voice loud amongst the eerie silence.

"Isn't it an AC/DC album?" Wagner asked, genuine curiosity in his voice.

De Souza stepped back and using a dial on his wrist quickly, shushed them, turning up the brightness on his own lights. At first the rest of his men were only able see the now familiar expanse of nothingness, then slowly they saw the shimmering ripple of black dancing across the ice.

"*Scheiße!*" Wagner cursed before clamping a hand over his mouth.

Nero ignored the man as he sidled up next to his friend and employer. "What you think? We're getting fucked?"

A small chuckle came from the other man, who quickly checked his wristwatch. "We're always getting fucked. That's the joy of being a merc. But we've got a job to do."

Turning, the two men cleared their throats and instantly the others went quiet. De Souza stared at them, his eyes taking in their expressions; a mixture of fear and trust, their postures, all straight and calm and De Souza's voice was all business. "It's a simple search and rescue op today, boys. We've got some scientists or researchers—"

"Which one is it?" Wagner's deep voice cut him off.

Nero's face was red and livid as he shouted, *You don't interrupt the boss!*"

It had been a while since any of them had seen Nero lose his shit at one of them. Sure, the man had gone off at cartel bosses, warlords, CEOs, and even the clergy, but for him to go off like that on one of their own? It was unnerving.

"Easy there," De Souza's voice broke the tension, and the leader turned his eyes back to the German. "No fucking clue, and honestly it doesn't matter. We get paid for each one we get out alive. And there is a hefty bonus for the wives and kids. So, to put it bluntly, gents, it's a fucking good payday."

There was a small cheer from the Filthy Animals, but it lacked any genuine enthusiasm. For some reason, each of them felt dwarfed by the isolation and emptiness they found themselves in.

Each man shared the feeling, and it kept them frozen in place. Even though they knew they had to get moving, there was a sensation of dread permeating everything. As if the ice was holding its breath, waiting for something tremendous to happen.

De Souza felt it too, but he pushed it to the back of his mind. He had a job to do and nothing would stop him from finishing it. Not even death would stop him, for his men would continue the work. "Snap outta it! We need to get moving." He read their minds.

Without another word, De Souza set off, following the edge of the wall of black ice. He kept one of the lights pointed at it and the other aimed at the emptiness.

Slowly, the rest of the team fell silently into line behind him, weapons at the ready. Fingers resting on trigger guards, their eyes scanned back and forth, watching the darkness vigilantly. And even though they couldn't see shit, it was better to be safe than sorry.

The field of black ice stretched on, seemingly never ending. There was barely any sign of life except for the six men trudging across the dark, creaking and cracking river. With each loud, bone-chilling sound, the men froze and waited. Following the sudden snap, a rumbling started, and for the trained mercenaries it could've meant a variety of things; a sudden drop into frozen oblivion, their limited world crashing in on them, or something from the depths rising up to tear each and every one of them to bloody piles of pulp.

It was the last idea that had taken hold of De Souza's mind. It was almost impossible to know where they were. Once they left the safety of the lights, stepping out of the halo there was nothing except for the faint glimmer and reflections bouncing off the ice. For the leader of the Filthy Animals, not knowing what he was leading his men into made him more cautious than ever before. He was positive that they had been fucked. All that remained to see was how much.

"You know where the targets are, right?" Nero's voice startled the other man, who gasped slightly. The second-in-command raised an eyebrow, the day was revealing more and more surprising things about the team. "Boss, all good?"

De Souza waved the question away and held up a small rectangular box. It was black too, except for an LED light blinking rhythmically. "Yeah, we're doing just fine," his voice was calm as he waved the device. "When the light picks up speed, means we're getting closer. So, all we have to do is keep going."

"But for how much longer?" The question hung in the air, and before De Souza answered, Nero fired off another one. "For that matter, what's the sitrep? Are we walking into another Tasmania?"

The memory of the worst job they had taken stampeded back into De Souza's mind and he shuddered before saying, "No. All we're doing is retrieving some scientists and their families. If anything should go awry, then we do what we do best. You get me?"

Nero nodded, then turned his head at the sound of a heated argument coming from behind them.

"This can't be Hell!" Wagner said while staring at the obscured expanse surrounding them. "Where's the fire and brimstone? What about the demons and the devil?"

Axel smiled and shook his head slightly. "Hel with one 'l'," he said then looked around too. "This is the perfect location for the realm of the goddess of death herself, Hel."

With a frustrated grunt, the German threw his hands in the air. "Make up your fucking mind! Is Hel a place or a person? At least in Christendom we have separate names for all of them."

"Helheim, is the realm. Hel is the ruler and daughter of Loki," Axel's voice was hushed as he spoke, his tone lacquered with reverence. "Depending on who wrote about it, Helheim is nothing but ice and darkness, with only the souls of the dishonoured dead to give any light." His eyes took in the other men, and he chuckled. "Of course, we'd be perfect for that role."

Still moving forward, the rest of the team were paying attention to the argument. Many a night was spent up late drinking and having varied and far-winding discussions about all facets of life. In the end, they would always end up blind stinking drunk. This topic had an urgency to it, like both were trying desperately to convince the other that they were right, and their faith was the sole path to salvation. That idea brought a smile to both Monette's and De Souza's faces.

"This," Wagner said with a gesture that took in all around them, "this is clearly Hell from Christianity. Specifically, the lowest level, Cocytus, the frozen lake that keeps traitors and fraudsters trapped forever. In the centre at Judecca, you'll find the Devil. Not some bitch from a Marvel movie, but the real deal. Satan, who isn't some buxom British sounding wench, but is, in fact, a three-headed monster that is also trapped and buried waist-high."

"A bitch?" Axel asked. His long-braided beard bristled at the insult to one of his goddesses, but he let it slide. He'd never seen his brother talk with such enthusiasm.

Wagner didn't hear the question and pushed on. "Satan has three faces and mouths, and is constantly chewing on Judas, Cassius, and Brutus. None of them will ever be devoured or die. Under each of his chins are a set of wings that constantly flap, forever keeping the frozen lake icy cold and trapping them more and more…what does your Helheim have?"

The question hung in the air as the Norwegian thought. He pursed his lips then went through his knowledge of Norse mythology and the tales his grandparents told him. Wagner looked at the others in victory. He finally won one against the theologist of the group.

Bringing up the rear was Fischer, the man's eyes darting about wildly. He stuck his tongue out slightly and steam rose from the tip. He didn't make eye-contact with the other members of the team. Something about this place had him on edge. The deep rumbling sounded again, and the man screamed, a shriek of pure terror that froze the others.

"Fischer! What is it?" De Souza bellowed.

Within nanoseconds the four other men had dropped to their knees, weapons up to their eyes, ready for killing.

"*Hurry!*" a small child-like voice filled the air. "Hurry! You can save us. Please?"

Monette spun on his knee, a section of black ice latching on to the fabric of his tactical fatigues. "What the fuck?"

The air was suddenly filled with a choir of voices calling out from the darkness, each one more desperate than the last. "My babies need you!"

"We are innocents!"

"They tricked us!"

"Daddy is scaring me!"

"It hurts!"

"My babies!"

"*Dooooon't!*"

The voices continued to cry out, panicked screams turning into anguished howls. Meanwhile, the team stood frozen in place. Their minds raced, conjuring horrific images that matched what they were hearing; children having their tongues torn out as blood erupted from their mouths, only to drown them. A father being disembowelled by his daughter, the girl wrapping his intestines around her own neck in glee before throwing herself from the upstairs balcony.

Each of the six men cringed, forcing their minds to other things. Family. Friends. The bartender with the big tits. But every time they did, the constant screaming brought them back to the now.

"Fuck this shit!" Monette bellowed before raising his weapon and squeezing the trigger. The roar of his weapon startled the other men, and the voices vanished.

As the rest of the Animals dove on to the slick wet field of black ice, Nero stalked over to the panicking man, grabbed the barrel of the weapon and raised his hand. The automatic rifle screamed to a halt as the man moaned and grabbed his face.

Monette stared at the second-in-command and an intense hatred flashed across his face. For a second, it seemed like he would attack the shorter man.

"You good?" De Souza's voice broke the tension and the two men turned to their commander. He stared at them both, his body trembling slightly, then glanced at the other three men. "Get your shit together, we're moving out. Now!"

Without waiting for a word of agreement, he turned on his heel and set off at a run. His right hand held the tracking device firmly in place while the left kept a steady grip on his weapon.

De Souza didn't care if the others followed. He needed to get to the targets as soon as he could. The briefing and the fuckers who gave him the job had forgotten to mention something that he considered need-to-know information. His eyes kept glancing down at the tracker, the light was flashing faster and faster now. He felt his pulse quicken to the point it was almost in synch with the device.

"You okay, Boss?" Nero's voice sounded distant and dreamlike.

The man kept pushing forward. Each step slipped slightly on the ice, De Souza grunting in annoyance. His frustration grew with each delay, and there was a nagging sensation, something tugging at the back of his mind. He couldn't figure out what it was, but he was more than certain it was fucking important.

"Boss?"

"I'm fine," De Souza mumbled as his eyes widened slightly. The light on the tracker was almost at the point of being constantly lit up. "We're almost at the target," relief filled his voice. He wanted—no, *needed*—the job to be over with and everyone back at HQ safe and sound. "How are the boys?" this came out as more of an afterthought and in fact, De Souza didn't really care. He knew they could handle themselves as well as any out there.

Nero's hand was firm as he squeezed his friend's arm. He held it until De Souza stopped moving and looked at him. "What's going on D?" his voice was filled with concern, albeit tinged with slight irritation. "There's something you're not telling me—what the flying fuck!?"

De Souza didn't hear him. He couldn't, nor did any of the others. All stood with the same slacked-jaw look of disbelief mixed with disgust and horror.

The ice wall looped around creating a cul-de-sac, each of the tiny lights helping to reveal the faintest hint of a curve. But what littered the frozen expanse of endless ice shook them to their cores.

"May God have mercy on us all," Wagner said as he furtively made the sign of the cross.

The surrounding air was thick and heavy with the stench of death. This was nothing new to the team. Each man could remember the first time they met death properly; in the army, on the force, walking down the wrong street, from a family member. But collectively they all were fast friends with death and destruction.

Axel's mouth filled with bile and the remnants of his lunch. Eyes stinging with tears, he fought the urge to vomit. Fischer, meanwhile, couldn't fathom the carnage on display.

None of them could.

"Put lights on *all* of it," De Souza's voice was low and solemn. Hollow, even. His men instantly set to work, unloading maglites, alongside tripods for LED lights to be attached and within a minute they were ready to see the full extent of the horrors. "Do it."

Each man turned on their light, the area suddenly illuminated by a halo of pale blue light. Dark pools of almost frozen blood dotted the area with the beams of light bouncing off the surfaces creating an eerie glow. Strewn throughout the crimson were body parts. Legs, arms, and torsos all had been violently removed, torn away from the others, and thrown aside without a care.

"*Min Gud!*" the Norwegian's voice cracked as the team leader drifted through the carnage. Each step was slow and measured, as if he didn't want to wake a sleeping baby.

"I need more light!" De Souza's voice was deep and sounded as if it came from out of a cave.

"Axel. Wagner. Monette," Nero ignored their complaints, the situation was well beyond fucked-up and the sooner they were done the—

"What the..." his boss' voice trailed off.

De Souza raised a hand in the air, pointed. It trembled, and the finger drooped slightly, almost as if it was afraid to point properly. De Souza's face was pale. He seemed on the verge of losing his lunch.

Heavy boots pounded the ice. Loud thuds, groans and cracking sounds were ignored as the team rushed to find out what startled De Souza so.

Their boots squealed on the ice, each merc sliding to a halt, eyes darting across the scene as their brains struggled to take it in; body parts were sewn together creating malformed abominations. Flaps of skin dangled from limbs creating obscene wings; organs draped around necks, wrists and heads like jewellery. From the flayed skin, drops of blood had frozen, forming crimson snowflakes and in some cases icicles.

"You've gotta be fucking kidding," Monette groaned as his mind refused to take in the full extent of the horrors before them.

Fischer gagged, turning away as he lost control of his body. He'd seen something similar back in Cambodia, but he convinced himself it was a nightmare. "They're true!" he muttered to himself. "Nightmares are real!"

Nero heard the ramblings and tore his eyes from a small girl. She was frozen mid-step, running in joy. Her body had been turned inside out, with the only hint of pain on her face being that of a silent scream coming from deep within her eyes. Her pure, innocent flesh laid on the frozen ground, tossed away carelessly by whoever had done this to her. Apart from the flayed skin, her exposed veins, nervous system, organs, and muscles, what truly horrified the man were the cocks sewn into her anus and vagina.

Something inside of Nero swelled, and he needed to punish whoever was responsible for the torture and death of this innocent.

He had to give her justice.

At any cost.

"Möge Gott uns allen gnädig sein! Denn wir waren Schafe zur Schlachtung und nichts kann uns jetzt beschützen!" Wagner's voice came out low and husky as he went between the defiled bodies, his hand performing the sign of the cross as he prayed for their souls.

It was clear to Nero that whatever happened, it was beyond the comprehension or reasoning of rational humans. But what was the aim? What could anyone have gotten from such depravity? As these thoughts ran through his mind, his eyes continued to take in the horrific sight before them.

A mass of limbs and genitals were bound with strands of sinew and stitched together with hair. These were shaped to resemble animals; a lion made up of legs and teeth, a pack of wolves made up of eyes, mouths, genitals, and assholes. But the *pièce de résistance* was a giant, this brute was nothing more than a mass of stitched together faces. Each one pulled taunt across unseen bulk and bones. Their eyes were wide open with the irises and pupils covered by a film that made them look glassy. Each mouth was stretched into a hideous grin that reminded Nero of a dog's snarl. The mass sent a shiver down his spine and then he noticed De Souza.

His friend and commander stood in front of a pile of discarded flesh. Slumped shoulders, it appeared as if he was on the verge of losing his shit. Slowly, Nero walked over to the man, ignoring the others as he made sure not to disturb any of the monuments to pain.

"D," his voice was soft, "what the fuck are we looking at?"

"The remnants of a failed expedition," De Souza's voice came out as if it was a machine and he pointed to the pile of flesh. "My brother's family were involved. That's why I took the job so easily…I should've told you upfront."

A part of Nero felt betrayed, but he understood; blood always came first. "No worries, Boss," he said with a gentle pat. "But what about the voices?"

That got De Souza's attention. Turning, he stared at his friend. His face was white, like he had seen a ghost. "You heard them too?"

Nero nodded, "We all did…What the fuck is going on?"

Monette's voice drowned out De Souza's reply, "Mates, you might wanna see this!"

De Souza and Nero turned to see the others gathered around Monette. The long-haired man had his lights pointing at something behind them and the two turned on their heels. Each one instinctively flipping the safety off on their rifles and placing a finger on the trigger guard.

Reaching out to them from behind the thick wall of ice, the six men could see sharp, jagged-edged claws the size of a man. Lights scanning the wall, their mouths fell open. It was almost impossible to tell how large *it* was…but looming over them, trapped behind the blackness was a demon; gigantic leathery wings fully spread gave it the appearance of a bat from hell. The body was heavy, not fat but definitely muscular and covered in thick scales, but it was the face that struck fear into each of them. Horns made from some unknown material erupted from the forehead and curved slightly at the tip, while the face itself was elongated to such an extreme that all the facial features were no longer distinguishable. The gaping maw reminded them of a snake's distended jaw and the rows and rows of teeth contained within were similar to that of a shark.

"How much intel were you given?" Nero's voice was small, even as it bounced off the frozen walls.

De Souza shook his head before saying, "The location, extraction point and the targets. Obviously, they thought this was above our pay-grade."

"What the flying fuck is that?" Monette said as he fought to control his bladder. There was something about this unearthly adventure that sent shivers down his spine, reminding him of a nightmare he'd never wake from.

"Satan. *Luzifer. Der Teufel. Wie auch immer Sie den Gefallenen nennen wollen,*" Wagner said, and the others turned to him. His voice was more like a preacher than a hired killer. "Isn't it obvious? We *are* in Hell."

Next to him, Axel laughed. It was boisterous, almost verging on maniacal. He turned to his brother-in-arms and said, "Pull your self-righteous head out of your ass! We're no more in Hell than we are in Scarlett Johansson's cooch!"

This brought forth a round of laughter from the others. Instantly they felt more at ease. It was good to laugh but there was something about hearing the sound fade away and slowly die—mixed with the scene before them—that made it seem perverse.

Free me!

The voice came from nowhere and everywhere at once. It shook the ground and made the Filthy Animals tremble.

"Mother of God!" Fischer's voice was a shriek as he felt something push at his consciousness.

Help me! Release me from my prison!

Beyond age, there was a desperation to it that reminded the men of a child's plea. But, like Fischer, the rest felt something probing at them, trying to dig in and latch on to a part of them. De Souza knew if it did that then they would be lost.

"What do we do?" Axel asked as he felt a stream of piss run down his leg.

Save me from damnation!

Now the voice sounded like a child's and the men gasped. It was the exact same voice they had heard earlier. But now, there was a strange quality to it, as if whoever was speaking didn't fully understand the language.

"*Odins skjegg!*" Axel whispered as he took a step back away from the frozen monstrosity.

I can take you to him!

"What the fuck are you?!" De Souza bellowed as he took a step towards the creature. "Are you friend or foe?"

I am all and neither. The Alpha and the Omega. The beginning and the end. Now, release me!

De Souza looked to Nero, then to the others. He had never seen them struck by such fear. Anxiety and nerves, yes. But abject fear was new, and it conjured a single emotion in the commander: an overwhelming desire to protect his boys.

Turning back, he took a step towards the creature and said, "Go fuck yourself!"

The voice bellowed, then roared its frustration, the entire plateau of ice trembling from the ferocity of it. Large, jagged cracks spider-webbed across the field towards the men. Their instincts took over. They dodged, letting the cracks circle the empty spaces.

Nero wiped sweat from his brow, then turned to De Souza, "What's the plan?"

"We destroy that fucking thing," De Souza said with a wolf's grin.

His hands moved rapid fire as he checked the magazine. It was full with hollow-point cartridges, and the sight made him feel more in control. With a satisfying click, the magazine locked in place and the skilled hand loaded the first round into the chamber.

Nero smiled. This was the De Souza he knew. A man who laughed in the face of danger and took life by the balls. "How do we do that?"

"Axel! Wagner! You guys got the goods?"

The German and Norwegian nodded and smiled. Reaching into their packs, the two pulled out small bricks of plastic explosives. Around them they could hear rumbling that reminded them of a dog growling. Whatever the thing in the ice was, it was getting pissed.

"What's the plan?" Axel's voice rung loud and clear, despite the cacophony.

De Souza waved his hand, getting the attention of the others and pointed at the wall of ice. "Blow it fucking sky-high!"

"Wait!" Fischer's high-pitched voice silenced the sound, all eyes going to him. "Are we sure that's the best idea? What if instead of destroying that thing, we unleash it? Isn't it better to just retreat?"

Nero and De Souza exchanged bewildered looks. Even though he was relatively new to the team, Fischer already proved himself to be a worthy asset. To hear him talk about turning tail and fleeing, it was beyond weird. De Souza glared at the man. "Why the fuck should we do that?"

Your doom is imminent.

Fischer nodded in agreement to the threat. "Who knows what other fucked up shit this thing can do?" He was shaking uncontrollably. Sweat fell from his brow, freezing in the air before then shattering as it hit the frozen tundra. "I for one, don't want to find out!"

Release me and I shall reward you handsomely. Refuse and your suffering will be worse than these unfortunates.

"*FUCK YOU!*" Axel screamed as he scrambled to his feet. With a war cry that sent a shiver down Nero's back, the man squeezed his assault rifle's trigger. His weapon roared, tiny bullets flying through the air and creating small indentations in the beast's prison.

Wagner and Monette joined him, their own weapons adding their voices to the scream of death and destruction.

Nero and De Souza glanced at each other. They both knew that this was a useless show of force. Even with the hollow-points, the ice wall was too thick for any actual damage to be done. All the three men were doing was wasting ammunition.

Does that make you feel better? In control?

"Fucking right it does," Monette cackled as his rifle clicked empty. Within seconds he had released the empty magazine and slid in a fresh one. The glint in his eye was one of pure hatred for the thing before them. Raising the weapon, he kept the barrel pointed directly at the beast's face.

"Cease fire!" De Souza's voice rung through the air. His men stopped immediately, the group looking to their commander, who got to his feet with ease. "Lower your weapons. Now."

The voice chuckled, a low sound that had the same timber and resonance of an underwater explosion. It continued to grow louder and louder until the six men felt the vibrations in their stomachs. Fischer groaned, gagged, then fell to his knees clutching his gut.

An acidic smell filled the air, and De Souza turned just in time to see the latest recruit lose the contents of his belly. As the malevolent presence continued its assault, the men strained to remain standing. None of them had ever experienced this level of force; not even in the heat of battle had they come across this and being bombarded by it now, made each of them terrified.

De Souza gritted his teeth, grinding them against each other as he pulled himself to his feet. His head felt four sizes too small, and the pressure was becoming more than he believed he could handle. The commander grunted and raised his weapon. His rifle silenced the oppressive noise, and all that remained was a dying echo and heavy breathing. The stunned men stared at him, and De Souza glared at the encased beast.

"Fuck you!" he spat before turning his gaze to his men. "On your feet! We're getting the fuck outta here."

No!

The cry shook the ground beneath their feet. It was almost impossible to tell how many voices were in the choir. At a guess, in the thousands.

Save us!

Each voice was wracked with pain, excruciating and never-ending that told of torture and pain never imagined being performed on them. Within the voices was a malicious chuckle and the wet, familiar sound of flesh being torn apart.

"What do we do?" Fischer's voice shook as he spoke. "We have to do something, right?" This was the question plaguing all their minds, but nobody had the answer. Not even De Souza, and that terrified the other men.

Yes! Save our souls!

Wagner laughed, pointing at Axel. "Told ya, pagan! *Souls!* This has to be Hell!"

"Shut the fuck up!" De Souza hissed. His eyes were focused on the frozen beast. He couldn't tell what was happening behind those pitch-black eyes, but in his heart, he knew something was coming.

Yes, you are in Hell.

The choir of voices had changed. No longer were they the mixture of men, women, and children. Now they were purring and deep, like the original voice trying to do an impression of humans.

Stay and save us!

De Souza looked to his men and shook his head. He had to buy them enough time for the pick-up signal to be sent. Once that happened, they were home free. Until that moment, every one of them had to tread carefully. He would not lose any men on this job. Of that he was determined.

Free me!

The voice came out frustrated and a loud, ugly crack filled the air. The men shifted uneasily, exchanging uncertain glances with each other.

Free me and I shall release them!

De Souza raised an eyebrow before looking at Nero. His friend and second-in-command wore an expression of disbelief which brought a smile to De Souza's face. Even in the field of black ice, the men could still be surprised.

Do not dare defy me!

The leader of the Filthy Animals turned back to the monster, stopping instantly. A dark, almost blood-red glow emanated from the beast. Its eyes were already glowing, and the man could hear a low growl that reminded him of wolves. De Souza's hand slowly tightened its grip on the handle of his weapon. Then his mouth fell open.

Nero, Monette and Axel turned, following their boss' gaze. They gasped at the sight of the glow surrounding the enormous monster.

But it was the slow shambling thing shuffling towards Fischer that really took the cake.

The mass of fused together flesh was moving! Each of the stretched faces blinked and groaned in hunger. The sewn together body parts that made up arms waved and bobbed with each step, an unholy fluidity to them.

"Fisch," Nero hissed, "turn the fuck around!"

"What? Why?"

Do we have an accord?

"Axel," De Souza said the name with all the authority he could muster. His voice snapped the blond man out of his stupor.

The hideous monster, blood and black ice dripping from its flesh, grew closer and closer to the mercenary. With each step the collection of mouths stopped groaning, instead growling and snarling with excitement and fervour. As it closed the distance between them, the thing swelled and a seam formed, running down the middle of the horror's torso.

"Axel!" De Souza bellowed as the creature's body split open with a sickening tear, revealing jagged teeth and a gaping maw. A long, man-sized tongue slithered out, licking at the skin closest to the teeth.

Fischer grunted then yelped from the cold and wet smashing into his face. The air left him. He fought to breathe under the weight pressing down on him, threatening to suffocate him.

A low growl drew the attention of the men, who all turned to stare at the obviously pissed-off monster. Its pulsating body, glowing with the same eerie energy as the beast towering over them, shook as it turned to look at its missing prey, then back to the other four men. A roar of unimaginable hunger mixed with anger filled their ears.

"That's just wrong on so many levels," Wagner said as he pulled the slide back on his weapon.

"Light it up," De Souza ordered softly, raising his own weapon and squeezing the trigger.

Tiny hunks of lead sped through the air, tearing into the screaming horror's bulk. Blood, chunks of muscle, sinew and bones flew into the atmosphere. The flesh erupted with tiny fountains of viscera that stained the frozen ground. The stuck together limbs flailed about as the monster's nervous system and body failed.

"Reload," Nero said as he let the empty magazine clatter to the ground. He didn't bother looking at the others, he was positive they were already doing the same.

You have chosen poorly.

Suddenly, the field of nothingness became filled with high-pitched shrieks mixed with creaks, cracks, and rumblings. It was as if the lake of black ice was breaking up and something worse was waking up.

"No shit, Sherlock," Monette said as he stalked over to Axel and Fischer. The large Norwegian was covered in tiny pieces of flesh, but he smiled proudly at his brothers. Wagner held his hand and looked as if he was going to cry while Nero and De Souza helped Fischer to his feet.

The man's face was white as a sheet. He seemed to have checked out. His eyes stared blankly into the emptiness, his mouth opening and closing of its own will.

Nero exchanged a concerned look with De Souza then motioned to Monette, "Help with this."

De Souza handed the stunned man to the other then turned to Wagner and Axel. "You boys okay?"

Both gave an eager thumbs up as the cacophony grew to the point of drowning out their voices. The men winced from the barrage, instinctively throwing their hands over their ears. Luckily, they had comms.

"What's the plan, Boss?" Wagner asked his, voice sounding distorted but understandable. Next to him, Axel nodded along looking like a big naughty puppy in need of attention.

"Blow that fucking thing sky-high!" their leader barked, pointing at the glowing monster. "Get me?"

The two smiled, then bounded over to the ice-wall. Their heavy boots crushed the ruined flesh as they pushed over the flayed girl.

"Is that going to work?" Nero's voice was soft as he stood next to De Souza.

The other man held up the tracker device. It was blinking blue and beeping rapidly. "Doesn't matter," he said. "All we need to do is buy us some time."

Monette's voice came through the earpieces, panicked and hurried. "Boss...ummm...what do I do?"

De Souza and Nero pivoted. Within nanoseconds their weapons were up, their eyes focused on the freaked out man.

"Fuck me," Nero sighed.

Fischer was still being held up by Monette, but now a dark black sludge was oozing from his mouth, ears, nose, and eyes. A repetitive moaning similar to a motor trying to start came from somewhere deep within his chest. He was shaking. Monette looked to the other men, his eyes pleading for help as the sludge climbed up his arms.

"Let go of him!"

"What the fuck do you think I'm doing?" Monette bellowed as the smaller man he held started to convulse. The sludge doubled its speed, hitting the ground with a dull wet thud before it snaked its way over to Monette's boots.

The man howled in pain as the sludge melded with his own flesh. It burned his skin and infiltrated his blood stream with ease. A second later the same sound that came from Fischer crept its way up Monette's throat.

"Jesus-Christ-On-Crutches!" Nero yelled as the sludge pulled Monette's trembling body further into the gelatinous form that had been Fischer. As the man screamed and howled, the air was filled with a deep chuckle that spoke of aeons of inflicting pain and receiving pleasure from it.

De Souza turned to where Axel and Wagner stood. The two men were busy going through their packs, hurriedly pulling out square after square of plastic explosives. His eyes darted up to the grinning face of the monster and he could've sworn it winked at him, the tiny movement somehow causing him to feel insignificant in the universe and at the same time question maybe all of this was for naught.

"Boss," Nero's voice sounded distant as he spoke, "what the fuck do we do?"

Hearing his friend's voice made the man feel somewhat in control but there was still a feeling of the job being a joke on a cosmic scale. He didn't know what to do about the melding abomination that was growing in size. Or how to save Fischer and Monette. All he knew was that they had to get out of Dodge quick.

Then he heard the high-pitched girlish laughter.

"What the fuck is that?!"

Spinning in place, both Nero and De Souza saw the skinless girl skipping towards the two startled demolitions men. Blood flew with each swing of her arms and her internal organs, now on the outside, threatening to snap from the tendons and sinew holding them in place. Her mouth was open in a perpetual scream. Yet, she laughed gayly, as if nothing was wrong.

Axel spun at the sound and instantly puked. His body heaving with disgust at the sight of the child happily pulling one of the cocks from her body with a wet, sickening tear of flesh and brandished it like a cudgel.

"Put that fucking thing down!" De Souza roared at his men before turning back to the melting monstrosity before him and Nero.

At the sound of their boss' order, Wagner turned and almost shat himself. The little girl was meters away from them. Now she had both members in either hand. She swung them around like nun-chucks. Albeit nun-chucks with tiny slithers of stale cum flying from the tips, splattering her face with flakes of off-white.

"Fuck that for a joke!" Wagner said as he raised his weapon.

The girl stopped dead in her tracks, both cocks dangling limply in her hands and the eyes rolled up into her head. Her laughter morphed into a whimper as blood ran down her face. The tiny figure trembled then slumped to her knees before screaming in pain. Her hands dropped the cocks then went to the bullet hole in her forehead.

Axel picked up a square of C4, casually inserted a detonator into it then tossed it at the screaming monster. The moment it connected with the girl he pressed the button.

There was a second of delay as the signal raced through the air, the explosion engulfing the undead girl. The force of the detonation sent flames, smoke, and gas into the air, tiny pieces of plastique tearing through flesh, at the same time sending organs and bone into the atmosphere. She was vaporised amidst a squelching sound mixed with the roar of the explosion.

The two men laughed as tiny pieces of monster rained from the sky before turning back to the job at hand. Each one knew what to do, and they set about finding the weakest points that would do the most damage to the beast within the ice. "Almost ready, Boss!" Axel called.

De Souza didn't hear him. He was too busy focusing on the creature in front of him. Monette's screams were gone as was Fischer's moaning. All that was left was the black sludge which had hardened and was now falling away. The man held his weapon at the ready, while balancing the tracker which emitted nothing but a solid blue light and a constant whine. He nudged Nero with his elbow then said, "Almost home free."

A bone-cracking, wrenching sound came from the shell, a twisted and mangled limb erupting from it. An arm and a leg fused together; the limb attacked the shell like a hammer. Each hit caused more and more of it to tumble away revealing the hideous monster the two men had become.

All shall become my children!

The voice invaded the four men's minds as the mutilated thing emerged from its cocoon. It was filled with desperation, sounding as if it was trying to sell the men its threats.

As the last remnants of the black shell crumbled, falling to the ice, De Souza and Nero saw what had befell the scientists and their families. The two men had been squashed together like they were made from clay; limbs twisted around one another in a grotesque game of *Twister*, blood oozed from the flesh and a groan of immeasurable pain filled the air.

"That's disturbing," Nero said.

De Souza had to agree with him.

Both men couldn't take their eyes off of the mashed together face, the mouths stretching together around the circumference of the skulls with teeth jutting out and tearing through the flesh. All four eyes aligned, they stared blankly at the men.

"Fucking kill it," De Souza sighed as he again squeezed the trigger.

Axel and Wagner heard a scream of pain mixed with gratitude that ended in a gurgle. The two risked a glance and saw the Monette-Fischer monstrosity clutching at its throat as blood squirted from the multiple wounds it had sustained. As the life left the creature, De Souza walked over to it, placed the barrel of his weapon against the thing's malformed head and squeezed the trigger.

"Get a fucking move on," the man ordered as he walked away from the corpse.

Nero was busy reloading his weapon as he said, "You okay, Boss?"

De Souza grunted as the shrieking returned. This time, though, it was closer than before and more violent. The sound was that of a horde of hungry animals all being tortured at the same time. "We're gone the moment they're done."

If only it was that easy.

The voice laughed, the wall of ice beginning to crack along its limbs. The shrieking slowly turned into a cooing and whimpering as the ginormous wall continued to break apart.

Rise up my children! Rise up and feast!

"Hurry up!" Nero yelled.

The ground shook, trembling as more and more cracks formed all around the men. Shards of black ice were thrown into the air as elongated and deformed arms punched through, gripping at the slick floor. With each new shaft, red light erupted forth, bathing the area in an eerie glow.

"Another five!" Wagner called while crawling up his friend's broad shoulders. He stuck his tongue out in concentration as he attached blocks of plastic explosives further up the wall.

"Now!" De Souza barked, opening fire at the throng of hideous monsters. In the distance he could hear chittering and slobbering as more and more of the unholy things crawled out of the caverns. Eyes darting about he did a quick count of the horrors rising to attack them.

"What the fuck do we do?" Nero's voice was a hushed whisper as the entire area was bathed in the same red glow that came from the frozen monster.

De Souza turned. A smile crept across his face. In the distance, he saw a spinning portal, it was their way home. "We haul ass and take as many of the fuckers down as possible."

Hope is the greatest enemy of your kind.

Ignoring the voice and its purr, the man double-tapped Nero's shoulder. "Keep them at a good distance."

A near-evil smile flashed across his face, then Nero took five steps, dropped to his knee and readied himself.

Turning to the other two men, De Souza made his way over to them. With each step, he swept his weapon back and forth in a wide arch, keeping the emerging terrors always in his field of sight. So far, all he could see were arms, legs and what could only be described as membranes that held engorged, diseased genitals.

"What's the fucking hold-up?" De Souza said. His voice made it clear that there would be no suitable answers.

"We don't have enough explosives," Axel spat then wiped his brow. Behind them, the three men heard the tell-tale sound of explosions and gunfire.

"But we've done the best we can," Wagner added. "This bitch should be dead and buried once we set it off."

With a nod De Souza said, "Holiday's over. Let's get the fuck home."

The two large men whooped and high-fived before a roar stole their attention. Spinning on their heels, the three men got a full look at the creature from under the black ice; muscles and bones exposed, the thing looked like a Hieronymus Bosch painting made real. There was something familiar about it, the way the shoulders flexed as it stalked towards them. It had the bearing and predatory movements of a lion.

"Fuck this," De Souza said before emptying a magazine into the beast.

Bring me their souls!

The command sent the creatures into a frenzy and they swarmed. As the horde of unholy abominations closed the gap between them and Nero, the man continued to throw grenades into the onslaught, taking pop-shots in between.

De Souza, Axel and Wagner formed a tight-knit huddle with their backs to one another. Slowly, they moved as one, spinning slightly and keeping their weapons high. Each time a beast came into range they squeezed off a shot, aiming for the head.

"Time to go!" Axel shouted at Nero. They were close enough so that the man could sprint to them.

"How you getting us out of this one?" the man asked as he fought to catch his breath.

"The moment this bitch blows, we haul ass to the portal," De Souza said with a nod towards the gateway. It pulsated with a man-made rhythm, humming mechanically.

"When are we blowing it?" Wagner asked as he took out another of the monsters. Dark red blood and viscera splattered the men who continued to creep towards their escape. Luckily, neither the monsters nor their master had noticed the swirling vortex.

"Now!"

Axel's finger pressed down on the detonator switch, a rumble sounding a second later.

The men spun, as did the monsters, all watching as a chain-effect of explosions went up and down the wall of ice. As each block of C4 detonated, more and more cracks spider-webbed out from the epicentre.

For a second, it appeared as if the wall would not fall.

"Moment it goes," De Souza whispered, "get moving. Last one through buys the beers."

Before any of the men could answer, an ear-piercing shriek broke through the rumbling and cracking as the ice wall imploded. Gigantic, sharp, dangerous, jagged-edged shards of ice tumbled down, piercing the flesh of the enormous monster.

The remnants of the Filthy Animals ran. Their feet pounding the ground as the horde of monsters charged towards their fallen master. Their shrieks of fright and anger trailed after the fleeing men, growing evermore frantic and furious.

De Souza glanced back, his neck cracking at the sudden movement. He watched as a cloud of dark dust and smoke engulfed the plethora of monsters. He smiled, even if the mission had been a failure, at least that thing from Hell was dead and buried. "Booyah!" he hollered as the portal grew closer. "Don't wait for me," he ordered. "Just get the fuck back home!"

The three other men didn't need to be told twice. One by one, they clambered into the floating portal, each disappearing with a slight pop. Only Nero remained with his friend and employer.

"What the fuck you doing?"

"Making sure you go through too," Nero replied with a cheeky smile. "You don't get to play hero today. Heroes get themselves killed. *Remember?*"

De Souza blinked then laughed while shoving his friend through the portal. He knew they wouldn't get paid the entire fee and it was most likely the reputation of the Filthy Animals would be tarnished. Jobs would dry up. But at least he got the majority of his men home safely and the world was saved.

Reaching up, he pulled himself into the portal. As his body started to be transported, he heard a deep, malicious laugh and the words, *See you soon.*

THE END

INTO THE GEYSERLAND

Lee Murray

Transported on the air, the probe pressed against the liquid barrier, oblivious to the sulphurous heat. A tiny pioneer, one among millions neither living nor dead, it thought nothing, felt nothing. Not anticipation, nor even dread, its mission encoded in its structure from the beginning of time. More often than not, the probes were lost, the carriers imploding into nothingness. But not all of them. Occasionally, a carrier would make contact, the explosion scattering the probes through the atmosphere in search of a landing site.

Like this time.

The probe's liquid carrier burst, ejecting it into the world where it settled on a blackened surface. Out of instinct, or something even more primal, the probe extended its spikes and found an unexpected entrance. There, it injected its contents, and, finding the conditions satisfactory, it began to replicate.

***

It was late afternoon when Taine swung down from the Pinzgauer, the thump of his NZDF-issue boots muffled on the tarmac. He surveyed the elegant façade of the old Geyserland Hotel complex and blew out a long slow breath.

Bizarre. This gig. This whole year. There was no other word for it.

He scanned the three-metre high galvanised wire fencing, the sort used for crowd control at cricket matches, its perimeter patrolled by military security, and shook his head. Situated on the rim of the geothermal valley, the hotel looked more like a prison than a world-class tourist destination. Albeit a comfortable one, with good quality mattresses, high thread count linen, streamed movies, and gourmet meals courtesy of the New Zealand Government.

With a scuff of gravel, Corporal Shane 'Hairy' Harris appeared at Taine's shoulder. "At least the accommodation's a step up from our usual arrangements."

Alongside Hairy, Private Matt Read snorted. "No kidding."

"I booked a weekend with Jules here," Taine said. "Before the pandemic hit. Had to cancel." He shrugged. With the lockdown, and the military called in to support the Government's COVID-19 response, he hadn't seen his girlfriend, Conservation Department biologist, Jules Asher, for months now.

Eddie 'Lefty' Wright was the last to join them at the perimeter. "Do you think they'll let us order room service?" he quipped.

Taine strode towards the gate. "Let's just focus on the job, shall we?"

Read mock groaned. "Yup. Another delightful babysitting assignment."

A curtain twitched and a woman's face appeared at one of the lower windows, her brow furrowed, and her jaw set tight. Taine's men might not love the assignment, but how must it feel being incarcerated by a military sworn to protect you?

Taine exchanged salutes with the private standing guard at the gate. "Sergeant McKenna, reporting for duty."

The soldier unlocked the gate, letting the four of them through and re-locking the gate behind them.

"Shouldn't we be bringing our guns?" Read asked.

"Nah," Lefty replied. "Who are you planning on shooting? The people in this hotel are New Zealand citizens, not enemies of the state."

"Sergeant McKenna!" Army medical officer, Jugraj Singh, strode out of the hotel lobby and across the car park to greet them. Taine knew it was him, the medic's gait and his voice the giveaways, since his face was all but covered with a blue surgical face mask.

Ever impulsive, Read stepped forward. "Jug," he said, extending a hand, but Jug pulled up, hovering at a comfortable distance.

"Whoops. Physical distancing. I forgot," Read mumbled, belatedly recalling that Jug wasn't part of Taine's immediate section, and therefore not part of their NZDF 'isolation bubble'. It was still hard to get used to, especially when it came to friends.

"There's a problem," Jug said, without preamble. "An escapee. Two actually, but luckily Sergeant Meyer's guys caught one as he was squeezing through the perimeter fence. The other, a fellow called Tim Johnson, has been gone about a half hour. Meyer sent some men after him. Here's hoping they've caught the idiot by now."

Taine stifled the urge to curse. What a way to start the shift. Didn't the escapees realise it was just prolonging everyone's agony? "You'd better show us where they escaped from," he said.

Leaving the rest of the section waiting in the parking lot, they followed Jug past the entrance to the basement garage and on through the gardens of hibiscus and hebe to the hotel's inner courtyard, where two soldiers were examining a line of knotted sheets dangling from a second-storey window.

"You're kidding me," Lefty said under his breath. "They climbed down a sheet-ladder? I thought that only happened in comic books."

Despite the two-metre gap, Jug caught the private's comment. "Being cooped up for an extended period can be hard on a person's psyche," Jug said. "So we've been using this courtyard as an outdoor exercise area, allowing guests out for an hour or so each day to get some fresh air. Meyer's been vigilant; he's had his section out here patrolling the perimeter continuously throughout the day, but in the evenings, when everyone is indoors, they dropped the frequency to every fifteen minutes."

Taine nodded. That seemed reasonable.

"Except our escapees, both on day thirteen of isolation, knew that. They waited until the patrol frequency dropped off before climbing down the building."

"Maybe they just didn't like what was on tonight's menu." Lefty chuckled.

Taine frowned. This wasn't a joking matter.

"Sergeant!" Jug called.

The sergeant, a blocky sort, turned to face them. Meyer. McKenna had met him once before, knew him to be a competent, no-nonsense soldier. That this had happened on his watch would irk him.

"Sergeant Meyer," Taine said with a nod.

Meyer waved away Taine's verbal salute. "McKenna. I see you've heard about our little SNAFU in progress." He pointed a chiselled chin at the rope ladder.

"Strange times, Sir," Hairy said.

Meyer nodded. "They are, indeed, Corporal."

"Has Commodore Webb been advised?" Taine asked.

Meyer arched an eyebrow in confirmation. "And the Director General of Health."

"The press?"

Meyer's lips were a thin line. "Unaware, at this point. We'd like to keep it that way until we have more information."

No kidding. Already, there was an uproar about the Government bringing in the army. Taine could only imagine the press' reaction if they got wind of a cock-up like this. A field day, most likely. Meyer's reputation would be mud, and the NZDF's by extension.

Now it was Taine's problem.

"We've isolated one of the escapees," Meyer's corporal said. "A man called Dave Berry. He's inside, spouting off about the affront to his rights and so on. It doesn't seem like the pair had any plan other than to scarper. According to Berry, Johnson doesn't have family or other obvious contacts in the region who he might run to."

"He could be lying," Hairy said.

"Could be," Meyer's corporal agreed.

"What I don't get," Read said, "is why run at thirteen days? Another 72 hours and they were home free."

Meyer's corporal clucked his tongue. "And why the sheets? It's not like returnees are locked in their rooms."

"Maybe they were trying to make a point?" Hairy suggested.

"Or maybe one or both of them returned a positive COVID-19 test on day twelve. They'd be facing another fortnight's isolation." Taine turned to Jug for confirmation.

But the medical officer only grimaced. "Sorry, Boss. I'm not allowed to comment on individual test results."

"It's a good theory, though, right?" Meyers prompted.

Jug paused, his gaze shifting to the fuchsia-gold of the sunset. He kicked at the curb bordering the garden bed. "I'd say it's a good theory."

At that moment, two soldiers in the latest NZ MTP smocks jogged into the courtyard, their faces flushed, and their hair slicked with sweat.

"Privates Landers and Ng," Meyer's corporal said as the pair ran across the grassy area. The soldiers pulled up, close to Meyer and his corporal, but distanced from Taine and his men.

"Ng? What happened?" Meyer said.

"We lost him in the Whakarewarewa Forest, Boss," Ng told his commanding officer. The other private, Landers, was still doubled over, his hands on his knees as he dragged in his breath.

Taine sucked in a breath, too. Finding Johnson would be tough. Bordering the lakeside town and the bubbling geothermal valley, the Whakarewarewa Forest, with its bike and running trails, was spread across 5,600 bush-clad hectares.

"He went to ground somewhere off the Yellow Track," Ng went on. "We figured we'd better come back for reinforcements."

Still panting, Landers straightened. "And some NVGs."

Taine nodded. It'd be dark in an hour; night vision goggles were a good call. But Meyer's men were off the clock, and the protocol was clear about sections keeping to their respective bubbles. It would be up to Taine's section to find and retrieve Johnson. The only good news was that the forest was so large that the chances of Johnson encountering a member of the public was limited. Taine turned to Lefty. "Eddie, you and Read take Miller, Weiss, and a couple of others. Find and bring back Johnson and anyone he may have come in contact with." He swivelled to face Ng. "The Yellow Track, you said?"

Ng nodded his assent.

"Yellow Track. Got it," Lefty said.

"And wear protective gear!" Taine said as the pair peeled off, heading for the parking lot. "Johnson could have the virus."

"Right, Boss!"

"Sorry to land you with this shit-show, McKenna."

"Not your fault, Meyer," Taine said as his men jogged out of the courtyard. Behind him, the knotted sheets thumped gently against the wall.

***

His corporal at his shoulder, Taine stalked down the fourth-floor corridor to the room adjacent to the stairwell where Johnson was being held. "Read. Miller. What's going on?"

"We don't know, Boss," Read said, shuffling his feet. "Johnson's been thumping on the door, screaming at us to let him out."

"What is it with that guy?" Hairy said. "He's already escaped once today. You'd think he'd want to keep his head down with all the trouble he's facing for his little unauthorised jaunt."

"It took us ages to catch him, too," Miller said. "Had us earing through the bush after him, and then weaving between the sulphurous pools. I nearly passed out from the stink!"

"And now he's keeping everyone awake," Hairy said. "It's 2am!"

"He sounds really scared," Read said. "Maybe he took some drugs or something?"

"He'll be trying it on," Hairy said.

But on the other side of the door, Johnson's muffled shriek curdled Taine's blood.

"Please. Dear God. Let me out. They'll kill me. Please, please!" He pounded on the door with something. A chair?

"Jesus," Hairy whispered.

Miller frowned. "I reckon he's playacting. There is no 'they'. I escorted Johnson into the room myself, and the only thing in there with him was that slippery mate of his, Berry—unless you count the folded towel rabbits."

Behind the door, Johnson howled again, his groan drawn-out and anguished.

"That's not playacting," Hairy said. "Could be he's having some kind of mental breakdown. Maybe—"

Abruptly, Johnson ceased his screaming. There was silence, followed by a rasping shriek, high pitched and eerie, like the creak of branches in the forest canopy. Or fingernails on a chalkboard. The noise was regular, strident. Taine shivered.

"What the hell?" Hairy said.

With no security cams inside the guestrooms, there was only one way to know.

"You'd better step aside, Miller," Taine ordered, and adjusting his mask, he swivelled the barrel on the chain-link bike lock, their temporary solution for containing the escapees until the police arrived in the morning. The lock clicked open.

Taine swung the door aside.

His stomach plummeted into his boots.

There was no sign of Berry. His back to Taine, Johnson was on the floor, one leg a mess of blood and bone. He held a chair in front of him like a lion tamer holding back…a…wētā.

Wētāpunga! Three giant crickets. Except when people called them *giant* crickets, they meant as large as mice, not the size of a small pony. One of the monstrous insects lounged on the bed closest to the wall, another dangled from the drapes, its sickled barbs hooked through the fabric, while a third, perched on the desk, gnashed a pair of thick black mandibles, its thorny rear limbs dripping in blood. Their collective antennae swished whiplike about the room.

Taine blinked, a split second while his heart insisted what he was seeing wasn't happening, wasn't *possible*. Yet Taine had seen plenty of other things that weren't possible in his thirty-six years on Earth.

"The fuck," Miller breathed behind him.

Miller's curse was pretty good evidence Taine wasn't seeing things.

The wētā on the bed thrust its rear limbs into the air, rubbing them against its massive thorax, the screeching stridulation making Taine's bones ache. The curtains picked that moment to tear, the velour shrieking in protest. The fabric gave way, and the heavily armoured wētā thudded to the floor, its antennae waving and its mandibles snapping dangerously close to Johnson's good leg.

Johnson scrabbled backwards. "Please! Help me!" he screamed.

Taine grasped the man by his shoulders, his fingers gripping the fabric of Johnson's shirt, and dragged him from the room, Johnson only releasing the chair when it stuck fast in the doorframe.

"The stairwell now!" Taine roared, still backtracking with Johnson, the man's leg trailing blood across the Geyserland's bespoke carpet.

Read and Miller leapt away, and, seconds later, Taine heard the fire doors open, felt the rush of cold air from the stairwell on the back of his neck.

"Hurry!" Read urged.

"Get the fuck out of there," Miller yelled.

Taine glanced up. Standing flatfooted, Hairy was staring into the room as first a wiry antenna, then a black serrated forelimb, reached through the door. The stridulation came again. The door on the opposite side of the hall started to open...

One of the civilians was planning on leaving their room. But with his hands full hauling Johnson, there was nothing Taine could do. "Hairy!"

The shout was enough to mobilise the former policeman. Hairy yanked the door closed. "Stay in your room!" he hollered at the occupant, his tone demanding compliance. "Bolt the bloody door and don't come out!"

It worked; over Johnson's blabbering, and the monsters' keening, Taine caught the clunk of the lock. Hairy dived for the stairwell, just as Taine heaved Johnson through. Miller and Read slammed the doors.

One by one, the giant wētā clambered over the chair, spilling into the corridor.

"Miller, get Jug up here," Taine said. "Tell him to bring his kit," Miller took off down the stairs. "Tell him it's Johnson; tell him—" What was he supposed to say? That three disciples of the God of Ugly Things were roaming the corridors. Who would believe it?

Read stooped to help Taine with Johnson. "No! Don't touch him," Taine said. Deep gouges in the man's lower leg revealed glimpses of bone through the sheared flesh. There was so little known about the virus. Johnson's body fluids might be just as contagious as any respiratory droplet.

"But Boss, he's going to bleed out," Read said.

Beneath Taine's fingers, Johnson was trembling with shock.

"Incoming," Hairy murmured.

Taine snapped his head up. All three giant wētā were approaching the fire doors, their antennae whipping in a macabre dance. Following the scent trail left by Johnson's blood? Taine ducked out of sight, below the level of the wired glass.

Johnson shuddered and went limp.

Turning, Hairy leaned his weight against the door. He slithered down the timber. "And you Kiwis insist there's nothing dangerous in New Zealand," he said. "Give me a nice little Australian taipan any day."

The door rattled, hinges creaking.

Hairy's weight wasn't going to be enough. "We need to do a better job of securing these doors." Taine twisted his body to lean Johnson up against the wall, and scanned the corridor for something they could use, but Read was already on it. The private yanked an artsy metal oar sculpture off the wall. He tossed it to Taine, who stepped over the pooling blood to thrust it through the door handles. Who said the arts had no value? Not exactly what the sculptor had in mind for his installation, but it did the trick. Just in time too, because the heaviest of the wētā was charging towards them. Taine's heart pounded with every ragged footfall. Alongside Hairy, Taine put his shoulder to the door.

He held his breath.

The monster flung its massive, armoured head at the door like a battering ram. The door rattled but held.

The creature's antennae whipped past the window. Snaked under the crack in the door.

Fuck!

Hairy shuffled out of reach. Taine repositioned his feet, stood his ground. Waited for the next onslaught. But the creature turned away to join the others. They moved off to explore, antennae whiplashing around the corridor. Taine prayed the hotel guests stayed in their rooms.

"McKenna!" Jug called, the limp the doctor had sustained in the Urewera ranges barely noticeable as he ran up the final flight of stairs, two civilian medical staff in his wake. Both dressed in PPE, one of the pair carried a stretcher.

Taking in the scene on the landing, Jug quickly dropped to one knee, and, throwing open his bag, he ripped apart the packaging of a large gauze bandage and slapped it over Johnson's leg. "What did he do? Try to kick his way through the window?" Applying pressure to the pad to stop the bleeding, Jug began wrapping the wound while the medical staff unfurled the stretcher.

"Um...there was a breach in security," Taine said. He glanced through the wired glass. The giant insects had turned into another corridor. "Hairy, can you get downstairs and check the hotel security cams?" Taine said. He gave his corporal a hard stare. "Keep an eye on the corridors. If the...threat...is still lurking in the building, it would help to know where. We don't want them encountering anyone else..."

Hairy got to his feet. "I'll check it out."

Taine tapped his headset. "You need to speak to me; use the comms."

"Got it." Hairy dashed off.

With Johnson's wound covered, Jug gestured to the corridor and the lifts. "We need to get Johnson to the hotel medical bay, so I can suture these gashes—"

Taine moved aside, revealing the sculpture oar jammed between the handles of the fire door.

Jug raised his eyebrows then turned on his heel, blocking the view from the staff. "On second thought," he said, "given who the patient is, and what we know of his status—" He nodded knowingly at his offsiders. "—I think it will be safer for all concerned if we use the stairs. Go now and I'll join you in a minute."

The pair didn't argue.

"What's this about, McKenna?" Jug asked when the pair were out of earshot.

"If you want an educated guess, I'd say it's another relic left over from the Jurassic," Read said.

Jug shook his head. "What are you talking about, Read?" But seconds later, his eyes flashed, realisation dawning. "No," he said slowly, "that's not possible. There was just one. Jules Asher assured us; she said that giant tuatara was a freak of nature. And anyway, you dealt to it, McKenna, you and Trigger—"

Taine raised his hands. "Doc, doc. Don't worry. It's not a Sphenodon."

At that instant, one of the creatures crossed the hall at the far end of the corridor, its shadow creeping across the wall, like a scene from a B-movie.

Jug shrank away from the fire doors. He wiped his face with his hands. "No, no. I don't believe it. Those were—"

"Wētāpunga," Taine interrupted. "Giant wētā. Yes."

"To be fair, they're not usually that big," Read muttered.

"We need to go back for Berry." Taine checked the corridor. "He's still in the room we pulled Johnson out of. He could be injured."

Jug swallowed hard, then nodded.

Taine yanked the sculpture oar out of the slot and opened the door, brandishing the blade in front of him. "I'll take point," he said drily.

They dashed across the corridor. Inside Johnson's room, the carpet was a mess of bloody whorls.

"Don't touch anything," Jug warned.

"Any sign of Berry?" Read called from the doorway, the private keeping one eye on the corridor.

"Nothing yet," Taine said. There were no other wētā either.

The bathroom door was ajar. Gesturing at Jug to stand back, Taine pushed it open with the oar, then jumped back. Nothing happened. "Berry?" Taine swished the shower curtain with the tip of the oar. Apart from a pile of twigs and muddy sodden towels on the floor, the room was empty.

"I think he's here," Jug said, his voice shaky.

Taine turned. The medic was looking down the gap between the beds. "Where?"

Jug pointed.

Taine gritted his teeth. Beneath the valance were the grisly remains of a severed ear. Taine shouldn't have put the padlock on the door. Berry was a *citizen*. He didn't deserve this.

"Boss," Read said quietly. He stepped into the room and closed the door, pushing the bolt across. At the same time, Hairy's voice crackled in his ear. *"McKenna, they're coming back."*

Taine signalled to Read and Jug to take shelter in the bathroom, then, his heart thumping, he stepped up to the door and peeked through the peephole. The floor rumbled; the fish-eye lens revealed nothing but darkness.

A blur of yellow raked by. Taine leapt away, his heart spiking so hard it hurt. What he'd thought was darkness had been the wētā's jet-black compound eye. The giant insect crashed on the other side of the door.

The sound of splintering rang out. Was the wētā breaking into the guest room across the hall? His grip firm on the oar, Taine crept back to the peephole.

In the corridor, a monstrous serrated leg burst from the insect's translucent carapace, the hook at its tip grasping at the air. It was breaking free of its casing. *Moulting.* With a hiss, the creature shifted inside the exoskeleton, the shiny new armour underneath cracking as it expanded.

Taine sucked in a breath. In his ear, Hairy did the same.

Stretching in what must be the wētā version of a downward dog, the creature kicked away the remains of its former skin. It had just doubled in size. If it wasn't so horrifying, it would be beautiful. But the skin, thick as leather, was obscuring Taine's vision. He pushed his face to the door, relieved to see the beast lumbering back down the corridor, its bulk now half the width of the hall.

"*You're all good. It's headed into the south wing,*" Hairy's voice said in his ear.

Read and Jug emerged from the bathroom.

"Any guests in the corridors?" Taine asked them.

"None so far."

Taine unbolted the door and pulled it open. He used the oar to push aside the discarded exoskeleton. It was like a malodorous crumpled parachute, its musky stench making his stomach roil.

Read closed the door to Johnson's room after them, pocketing the chain-link bike lock. "I should have believed the man. Let him out earlier. All the time he was watching these monsters rip his mate apart."

"You couldn't have known," Jug said. "Berry may have got the better of it; who knows how the trauma might affect Johnson. Assuming he survives the virus…"

"Jug, if Johnson tested positive and he carried the wētā back from the forest on his clothes, could the virus have altered something in their physiology?" Taine asked. "Could this be our first contact with a new species?"

"Well, *something* definitely happened," Jug said.

Out of habit, Taine fingered the flattened wood pūrerehua-bullroarer that hung at his throat, wishing he could contact his old mentor, Rawiri Temera. There was a time when just touching the musical instrument could connect him with the wairua-spirit of that irascible old man. But Taine's friend was dead and beyond his reach, having made a deal with a pair of fire demons to save Taine's life. Maybe those same demons Te Pupu and Te Hoata, who once carried volcanic fire from Hawaiki to their chieftain-brother on the frozen flanks of Mount Tongariro, knew something of the wētāpunga. The goddesses had been known to pop up occasionally with warnings for Taine's friend. Although, their intent hadn't always been altruistic...

Read kicked at the discarded leathery sheath. "Maybe the gases near the geysers mutated the virus? Don't the local Māori say that taniwha live in the geysers?"

Jug grunted. "We know so little about it..." He shook his head. "Let's say it was the virus that did this; to cause the wētā to grow that big, and so quickly? The insects must have moulted before now. Where are the other skins? The other *insects*?"

"Eaten?" Read suggested.

Jug paled.

They didn't have time to stand around speculating. Sooner or later, someone was going to step into the corridor and when they did, the insects could attack again. Taine touched his mic. "Hairy, get Lefty's perimeter group to secure the basement stairwells, will you?"

"Already done, Boss. Lefty's in the basement now. I'm sending Miller and Weiss up with some ordnance."

Ordnance. Taine winced. The wētā might have killed Berry, but was that really their fault? Any creature would attack if it were cornered. And wētā were endemic to New Zealand. Endangered too. No matter how these giant bugs came about, they were unique. Jules would say they were a living treasure. A *taonga*. Temera might have said the same.

"I'd better see to Johnson." Jug headed for the stairwell.

To be fair, there wasn't much that could be done for Berry.

Watching Jug go, Taine spied the bucket-sized dent in the fire doors. Taonga or not, the creatures were powerful. Deadly. "When you get there, keep the door bolted," he called after the medic.

Turning back to the corridor, Taine raised his fingers to the pūrerehua-bullroarer once more, but the old man remained silent.

Instead, Hairy's shout rang out in Taine's earpiece. *"They're trying to get into one of the rooms!"*

Dammit.

Taine and Read sprinted down the hall, past the bank of lifts, to where the corridor diverged.

"Which wing?" said Read, his hand on his headset.

"Go left, then left again. It's the south wing, Room 466," Hairy's voice was calm. *"I think someone must be moving around in there, making a noise or something."*

They dashed to the junction, Taine grabbing Read and pulling him back by his tunic before he raced headlong into the south corridor. The private had a habit of being impulsive. "Softly does it," Taine said.

They peered around the corner.

The largest of the insects, the one with the single spike protruding from its rear, was pummelling the door with its massive head.

"Where's Miller with the guns? Those hinges aren't going to hold," Read whispered.

The wood whined in protest with each thundering collision. Taine shuddered too. Whatever had happened with Berry and Johnson, this time the wētā weren't cornered. This was predatory. They wanted to devour the morsel inside. How long before they realised that there was a tasty human, and sometimes two, in every room? The hotel would become the monsters' chocolate box.

Behind the door, a woman cried out. No doubt she'd put her eye to the spyhole and seen the nightmare on the other side.

"We can't wait. We'll have to draw them off."

"Right," Read said. Before Taine could stop him, he leapt across the hall, hitting the light switch, and flicking the lights on and off, on and off.

The wētā turned in their direction. Taine had to admit it was a good ploy: Read had attracted their attention, stopping the pounding before the creatures woke the entire floor.

Except now Read had their attention. "Whoops." He took a step back. "Any suggestions for what we do next?"

"The lifts. Go!"

They spun on their heels and charged for the bank of lifts, turning right, and right again. Younger than Taine by more than a decade, Read reached the lifts first. He thumbed the button to call the elevator. Danced on his toes to dissipate his nervous energy. As the lift stirred itself, they surveyed the corridor.

Nothing yet, but the floor thrummed, the vibrations revealing when the heavily armoured beasts slowed to take the first corner...

Where was the lift? Taine flicked his eyes to the call panel. The car was still on the third floor!

"Come on!" Read punched the button again.

Seconds passed as the car crawled the final few metres, the grind of the gears dopplering in the lift shaft.

"Boss," Hairy warned. "They're here."

He was right. The wētā were crowding the far end of the corridor. If anything, they looked even bigger. Taine's adrenaline surged. He fought the urge to turn and run.

The size of those black mandibles!

Each one was like the Grim Reaper's sickle. No wonder the Māori called wētā the devils of the night.

The lift trundled upwards.

"Take the damned stairs," Hairy said.

A door clicked behind him. Taine's heart lurched. *Please don't let it be a guest leaving their room.* He whirled, then whirled again. Not a guest; it was Miller and Weiss. They'd taken the stairwell nearest Johnson's room and were emerging through the fire doors. Weiss had lifted his Mars-L rifle, letting Taine know that they were armed. But they couldn't fire at the wētā. Not with Taine and Read in the way.

With a ping, the elevator doors began to trundle open. Too slow! Even if Read and Taine made it inside, would the doors close in time? They could be trapped in the car...

"Read, top of the car now," Taine whispered.

Read didn't argue. He squeezed through the still opening doors and into the lift, punching the hatch above his head open with his fist. Read swung onto the roof of the car, as fluid and flawless as a gymnast were it not for the bike chain tumbling from his pocket and clattering on the floor of the cab.

"*Boss,*" Hairy's voice was quiet in Taine's ear.

The beast's antennae spiralled through the corridor, one whipping past Taine's foot. Taine held his ground.

"Tell Lefty to stand by." He jumped into the lift.

"McKenna, come on!" Read thrust his hand through the hatch at Taine. Taine ignored it, instead stooping to thrust the oar between the lift's outer doors. Damn. He'd forgotten about the inner doors. He backed away, his foot striking the chain-link bike lock. Grabbing it, Taine crammed the chain into the door track, forcing them open too.

A shiny mandible curled around the door.

Taine snatched his hand back.

Time to go. Using his palm, Taine punched the button for the fifth floor, the car rising even as he leapt for Read's outstretched hand. Read caught him. The giant wētā's head loomed, huge in the doorway. It waved its fleshy yellow palps. Clacked its mandibles.

Dangling in the car, clinging to Read's hand, Taine reached for the lip of the hatch with his free hand. The cab continued to rise, the creature in the corridor falling away. In seconds, Taine would be beyond its reach.

"We're good," Read breathed.

"Lefty. Call the lift," Taine said, "Now!"

Read gasped. "What? No!" The private clamped two hands on Taine's upper arm.

Taine shrugged him off. "Stand down, Read." Both hands gripping the hatch, Taine ceased climbing, his body still swinging inside the car. He ran in place, his legs two worms dangling like bait.

The insect's compound eye flashed with malevolence.

Taine's spine tingled. Treasure or not, the wētā wanted him dead.

With a hiss, the colossus lunged. The scissored mandibles snapped for Taine's feet...and missed.

The giant insect plunged into the lift shaft, just as the elevator lurched, reversing direction. Weighed down by its enormous head, the insect grappled to save itself, flinging its serrated legs at the walls, the cab, at Taine... A single giant hook caught inside the car; now the wētā, like Taine, was dangling, only it was travelling on the under-side of the cab.

Sucking in a breath, Taine engaged his stomach muscles and swung his body onto the roof of the cab alongside his private, the manoeuvre not as easy as it used to be. "Hang on!" he told Read as he gripped the chassis of the cab and braced himself for the ride.

The car plummeted.

Four...three...

Taine fixed his eyes on the hook. Prayed the elevator pit wasn't a deep one.

Two...one....

The creature's body scraped the inside of the lift shaft, producing the same wailing stridulation as earlier. Eerie and horrifying. At last, the lift slowed to a crunching stop. All at once, a sickening wave of musk invaded the cab and wafted up through the escape hatch.

Had they crushed it?

Taine peered through the hatch. Inside the cab, still wedged between the door frame and the lift shaft, the monster's back leg and its grappling hook tip shuddered.

***

The outer doors of the elevator slid open revealing a slew of Mars-L rifles in the mostly empty garage.

"It's us," Read said, jumping down through the hatch and sidestepping the wētā limb to join Lefty and the rest of the perimeter team.

Taine climbed down after him. "Thanks for calling the lift. We had some unwelcome company."

"Holy fuck!" Lefty lowered his rifle, his eyes widening at the sight of that hooked leg still quivering in the cab. "No kidding. What is that thing?" His eyes on the mangled limb, Lefty removed his Glock 17 Gen 4 pistol and handed it to Taine.

"A wētāpunga," Read said, slinging the strap of a spare Mars-L over his head. "An unusually big one."

"Boss." It was Miller. Taine's section members paused, all listening for the private's report. "The bugs are on the move. They're heading for the eastern stairwell."

Finally, a chance to contain the situation. "Keep your eye on them, Miller. Any threat to the guests, you have my permission to fire."

"Yeah, about that. Weiss took a shot at the monsters when you and Read jumped out of the corridor," Miller replied. "Even Weiss couldn't miss a head shot. Problem was it didn't make so much as a dent in its black ninja armour."

Taine's heart sank.

"They don't like it, though," Weiss added, in his expat US drawl. "It wasn't the sound, because I used a suppressor, but that one shot sent them scurrying, which is how we've been able to herd them towards the stairwell."

That was something at least. And they were *insects*. As big as they were, their brains had to be tiny. If they even had brains... "Let's move," Taine said, slipping the Glock into his waistband and striding towards the exit ramp. "We'll head them off in the stairwell. I'm going to give Jules a call; see if she can help."

Lefty grinned. "Give her a kiss from us," he said before jogging ahead.

The last to leave the basement, Taine looked for garage door controls, finding the panel near the charging station where a single Tesla was connected. Taine punched the button. The grill mechanism rattled for a second, then stopped. "Hairy. The garage doors. We need them closed."

"I'll get right on it, Boss."

Taine pulled out his phone.

Jules's voice was groggy with sleep. "*Taine? Is something wrong?*"

"I need your help." Taine jogged into the grounds, jumping a garden bed to keep up with Read and Lefty.

There was the sound of rustling, as if Jules were sitting up in bed. "*Must be important; it's nearly 3am.*"

"We've come across some wētāpunga. A new species."

"*Taine, that's amazing.*" There was a click as she turned on the bedside light. "*What makes you think it's a new species?*"

"They're bigger than any I've ever seen before."

"*Maybe they're cave wētā; they can be pretty big. As large as a kitten when their legs are extended.*"

Taine leapt over a moonlit curb. "These are quite a lot bigger than that."

"*Really? Then yes, that sounds like a new species. Is there a breeding pair? The females will be larger,*" Jules said, clearly fully awake now. Taine imagined the soft tangle of her hair falling over her shoulders. "*They have a single curved ovipositor protruding from the abdomen. Males have two shorter cerci.*"

"Two males," Taine said.

The female is crushed. At the bottom of a lift shaft.

"*I wonder if there are more. They tend to congregate in tight damp places called hotels...*" Taine almost laughed at the irony. "*...typically in forested areas, usually only coming out at night—*"

143

"Jules, they're *giant* wētā. Each one is the size of a bull."

On the other end of the line, Jules fell silent. Taine imagined her nibbling her lip as she processed the information.

"They've already killed a man. All that was left was his ear."

More rustling. When she spoke, her voice was even. *"What do you need from me?"*

"Our guns are ineffective. There are several hundred vulnerable citizens in this hotel, and another seventy thousand in the township. I need to know how to eliminate the threat."

"But if it's a new species; anything I tell you could be bogus. I was wrong about the Sphenodon..."

"Jules—"

"Okay, okay. Assuming they're like your regular garden wētāpunga, then they'll have ears on their knees, so if you take out their legs, and their antennae, then you've effectively blinded them." She paused. *"I guess without legs, you've effectively immobilised them, too. They breathe through their exoskeleton, carrying oxygen directly to their muscles. No, skip that. That wouldn't be likely if they're as big as you say. Definitely watch out for those back legs; they swing forward. Even the teeny ones can rip through skin. Those barbs—"*

"McKenna," Hairy's voice crackled a warning in his other ear.

"Jules, I have to go."

"Be careful," she whispered.

Pocketing his phone, Taine sprinted up to the fire doors at the base of the east stairwell.

"It's good and bad news, Boss," Hairy said. *"Our beasties have pushed through into the eastern stairwell, so they're on their way down to you. The bad news is there's someone up and about on the first floor. Sneaking out to the stairwell for a late-night smoke, I reckon."*

Damn.

Taine flung open the fire doors, Lefty and Read crowding in behind him.

"I guess we get up close and personal and squeeze off a shot between the plates?" Lefty said.

Read harrumphed. "Says the man who's only seen a leg."

Taine looked up into the tower and spoke into his comms, "Miller, Weiss. Secure all the doors leading to this stairwell. Use whatever you can find. Gilbert, you and McNaught block the doors behind us. Park a damned Pinzgauer in front of them if you have to. Whatever happens, we can't let these creatures out of the hotel."

Not waiting on a response, Taine charged up the stairs.

***

The guest was on the first-floor landing. Wrapped in a hotel dressing gown, he had his head down, his hands cupped around a match trying to light a cigarette. He hadn't seen the wētā, which were clinging to the railing just half a flight above him. Their shiny carapaces gleamed in the dim light of the tower.

"Oh cripes," Lefty said, clocking the creatures for the first time.

His comment alerted the man, who raised his head. Spying Taine and the rest of the section at the bottom of the stairs, he turned and rushed back to his room on the first floor.

But by now the wētā had swung onto the landing and were blocking his path, like a pair of sphinxes, one on each side of the fire doors. The man gave a squeak of shock and staggered back a step. Excited by the sound, one wētā scuttled forward, its antennae swooping about it, sampling the air. All at once it threw a serrated leg over its body like a scorpion brandishing its tail. It plunged the barbed tip into the man's hip and yanked him back towards its clacking mandibles as if pulling on a lasso.

The guest struggled, mewled, too terrified to scream. The monster held him fast, drawing him closer to those formidable blades.

Taine shivered. He had to do something. The wētā was about to shred the man, dragging him across the landing. Hotel slippers skidded on metal.

Taine raised the Glock and shot at the internal fleshy portions of the wētā's mouth. But the mouth was protected by those flailing mandibles and the bullet struck the armoured carapace and shied away, hitting the wall.

The creature barely flinched.

Enclosed in the stairwell, the blast had been enough to distract the beast, though, because it pulled the barb from the man's flesh, taking a rib-eye chunk of his hip with it, and slammed the rear leg down again, this time just inches from where Taine was standing.

Now its mandibles worked the piece of flesh, squeezing the jus from the meat.

But that spiked rear leg was still too damned close.

Taine leapt onto the rail, balancing on the metal balustrade, and took a shot, this time at a foreleg, hoping to destabilise it. The shot smashed into the limb, shattering the joint at the knee.

Read saw his advantage, ducking in and grabbing the injured man by his borrowed dressing gown, now soaked in blood. COVID-19 clearly the last thing on his mind, Lefty grasped the man's other arm.

One monster at a time.

Hissing in rage, the wētā dropped the bloody morsel and attacked again, balancing on its other limbs, and striking out again with its rear leg. Taine evaded the blow, dropping to his thigh to slide down the rail, where he landed on his feet several steps below Lefty and Read who were still dragging the bleeding man down the stairs, the metal structure thrumming beneath their boots.

Taine threw open the doors to the ground floor. Raised his eyes. Above him, the knee-capped wētā was still thrashing its rear leg at the spot where Taine had been standing just a second before. Meanwhile, the second monster gripped the rail with its mandibles, anchoring itself as it dragged its antennae across the blood on the stairs and over the chunk of human meat. It stridulated, rubbing its legs across his thorax.

Glee? Or perhaps frustration that there wasn't more.

Taine didn't wait to find out; as soon as Read and Lefty had pulled the man through the doors, he slammed them closed. "Medical bay—*go!* End of the hall. Singh will let you in," he said.

They took off, the guest supported in a fireman's lift between them. Taine stooped to grab the trailing dressing gown cord and used the fabric to tie a constrictor knot around the handles of the doors. At least, he hoped it was a constrictor knot; he hadn't had call to use one for a while.

By now both wētā had scuttled down the stairs. Taine slowed. Turned. Would they charge the door? Just how much had the insects learned in the past half hour?

The wētā seemed to know they were being tested. A compound eye peered through the wired window, and one of the creatures curled an antenna through the slit under the door. Taine backed out of reach. The slender appendage probed the bloodied scrap of dressing gown cord, either testing it or tasting the knot. Eventually, it withdrew. Taine expected the wētā to back up and charge. Instead, it gnawed at the doors where the handles met, digging the blades of its mandibles into the wood to create a small hole. Then it thrust its hind limb over its body, slipping the barb-tip into the gap between the doors.

Taine's heart did a flip. It was reaching for the fabric. The hole wasn't quite big enough yet, but give it a few minutes and it would be. The insect was *planning*. Strategising. In minutes, it would shear the fabric apart and when that happened it would simply swing open the doors. Without expending any energy. Or the colossal headache.

Taine turned to follow the trail of blood that ran past the bank of lifts to where Jug had just ushered the latest victim into the medical bay. Thank goodness, there were hardly any civilians on this floor of the hotel. Apart from a few ground-floor rooms reserved for disabled guests, now their security HQ, this level housed the shared facilities, including the dining room, laundry, and kitchen. He'd made it halfway along the corridor, when Weiss and Miller appeared at the far end of the corridor, just as Read and Lefty emerged from the medical bay, which in pre-COVID times had been the hotel's conference rooms.

"Where are they?" Miller said.

Taine signalled behind him. "At my six."

Miller raised his rifle and took a step back. Weiss did the same.

Taine didn't need to be told; the insects had broken through. And once again he was caught between his men and the threat.

He darted forward, fast and low, but an antenna caught his tunic, tearing the fabric at his shoulder. Taine shook it off. A leg scraped the wall beside him, the jagged barbs carving the wallpaper off like a shave with a double blade. Too damned close. Taine yanked open the nearest door and dived inside, tumbled to the left away from the entrance. His back to the wall, he whipped out the Glock, readying himself for the attack, but the door sheared off, the diabolical pair crowding past, their bodies scraping the walls of the corridor.

Of course. Why go looking in a cupboard for a snack when there were four out on the bench? The monsters were looking for easy pickings. Chasing his men. Maybe Taine could outflank them. But with what? The Glock hadn't made much of a difference even at close range in the stairwell, and it wasn't like he could let loose with a Carl Gustaf M3 even if he had one. Not inside the hotel. Try explaining *that* to the media.

That is, assuming we all live.

He glanced around the cupboard for something, anything, he could use against the wētāpunga. There were shelves of sheets and towels, extra waste bins, cleaning supplies, a box of toilet paper. Nothing which could serve as a weapon.

"Where are they?" Taine spoke into the comms.

"*The kitchens,*" Hairy said.

"On my way," Taine said. But he paused. On one of the shelves was a stock of insect bombs. Four cans. The normal domestic sort you set when you were planning to head away for a weekend. Fleas and bedbugs travelled on suitcases. Maybe the hotel had had an infestation of the creatures' smaller cousins. Taine grabbed a can. Seems the bombs worked on fleas and cockroaches and a whole range of crawly insects. Could it really be that easy? He checked the small print. "Insect growth regulator can take up to three weeks to achieve full effectiveness."

"*What was that, Boss?*" Hairy said.

"Nothing." Either it worked or it didn't. It wasn't like they had a lot of other options.

Taine tucked a can into each of his chest pockets and another into his pants. He pulled the tab on the final can, locking the spray mechanism in place and then, the bomb streaming, he ducked into the corridor and ran to catch up with his section.

The situation in the kitchen was completely FUBAR.

Weiss was on the floor, out to it, a purple bruise on his temple. At the far end of the kitchen, one of the wētā was busy moulting, which would have been the perfect time to neutralise it if the rest of his section weren't already occupied trying to save Miller.

The private had opened the walk-in refrigerator. Maybe he'd hoped to entice a wētā inside and trap it there. Instead, the wētā had trapped him, pinning the young man at chest level between the door and the doorframe, the wētā's razored mandibles forced up against the metal. The weight of the insect was crushing him. Cracking his ribs. Miller's face was dimpled blue. They had a minute, maybe less, before the pressure suffocated him.

"McKenna!" Read had his Mars-L wedged in the gap in the door and was frantically trying to lever it open, to counteract the monster's weight and give Miller space to breathe. The rifle buckled under the strain. The Lewis Mars-L was a good rifle, a step up from the Steyr, despite the initial firing pin issues, but no one had thought to test the barrel against an enraged wētā the size of a bull. Lefty had already worked that out and had darted under the smashed foreleg to shove a carving knife between two articulated plates at the creature's neck. But it was taking too long. Like sawing through drywall. Miller would be dead long before the blade hit the creature's brainstem.

"Lefty." Tossing his friend a can, Taine rolled under the creature's belly, coming up the other side.

"Fly spray?"

"Jules said they breathe through their exoskeleton."

"She means the little ones."

"You got a better idea?"

Taine heard him snort, then give the can a shake and crack the spray nozzle.

Crouching, his senses on alert for those slashing legs, Taine dragged in a breath, reached up and sprayed the liquid mist over the length of the creature's body. The fine white spray coated the black plates. He assumed Lefty was doing the same on the other side. Even through his face mask, the musky smell of the moulting wētā mingled with the chemical stench of the bomb. The gimpy monster hissed. Using its good legs as stabilisers, it lashed out with a rear limb, bringing it forward to smack the refrigerator door.

Read gasped with effort. Miller made no sound.

Still, Taine felt a glimmer of hope. The wētā didn't like the spray.

He yanked out another can, rolling it across the floor for Lefty. Then he smashed the lock off the final insect bomb and sprayed again.

The rolling aerosol never reached Lefty; the wētā stomped on it with its foreleg, puncturing it. Under pressure, the spray ejaculated into the kitchen, spattering Taine's tunic, and coating the insect's underbelly. Lefty was already back at his station, trying to force the blade between the armoured plates. Taine kept his finger on the spray trigger, slathering the insect's thorax with the toxic foam. The chemical was cloying. No doubt it was toxic to humans, too. Right now, it was the lesser of two evils.

There was a crack. Read's rifle had snapped.

Read moaned as the fridge door shuddered inward, Miller taking the full weight of the beast. The boy's head dropped.

Jesus.

Suddenly, the wētā staggered away.

"Miller?" The private wasn't moving.

Lefty leaped out of range of the wētā's razored legs. Taine slid across the floor, dragging Weiss clear as the beast lumbered off, smashing against the kitchen island, and then the door frame. It slumped to the floor in the corridor opposite the bank of lifts.

Taine looked over at the moulting wētā. It too had ceased moving.

The fly-spray had worked! It was a bloody miracle.

Tossing away the empty can, Taine brought his hand to the comms. "Hairy, we need Jug in the kitchen. *Now.*"

Read dropped to his knees. He tilted Miller's head back, opening his airway, while Taine checked on Weiss, who was finally coming around. The soldier had a cartoon-sized lump on his forehead and had likely sustained a concussion.

The medical bay was only metres away, so Jug arrived in seconds, squeezing past the mountain in the corridor to rush into the kitchen. He headed straight for Miller.

Read moved aside, getting to his feet. "Boss," he whispered, nodding towards the windows.

Taine turned. The moulting wētā was moving again, trying to kick free of the exoskeleton.

Dammit. Had it been playing dead? Taine had been sure it'd been affected by the spray. Perhaps the solidified carcass had protected it from the toxic mist. Or maybe the dosage was simply not enough unless delivered at point blank range. It didn't matter. They'd exhausted their supply. But those breathing holes were a source of weakness. What if they could be clogged up somehow?

Before the moulting wētā was fully free of its crumpled cocoon, Taine grabbed a can of cooking oil from one of the benches and shook it over the carapace. Gluts of the viscous liquid dribbled over the outdated wētā packaging. When the can was empty, Taine hurled it away and grabbed another, emptying the contents on the creature. A hairy palp raked his wrist. Taine jumped away. Would the oil inhibit the creature's breathing?

Read wasn't waiting to find out. The private ran in with a handheld cooking torch, pointed the flame at the oily carcass, and squeezed the trigger.

It whooshed alight and exploded into flames, sending out billows of grey smoke. Like all creatures confronted by fire, the creature panicked, charging about the kitchen, dragging the flaming carapace.

"Look out!" Taine dragged a groggy Weiss under a table.

Lefty leapt onto the kitchen island, and Jug and Read pulled Miller into the fridge to avoid the stampeding insect and its trail of fire. The door was mangled, but at least they were safe from slashing legs and gnashing mandibles. That was something.

The wētā howled, the vibrations turning Taine's marrow to jelly. Luckily, like most commercial facilities, the hotel kitchen was mostly stainless steel, the gas bottles were stored outdoors, and Taine had already used all the cooking oil, so there wasn't much else to catch alight. Just a wētā, roasting in its skin. In minutes, the flames had consumed it, blackening the carcass even further.

The hotel sprinklers started, activated by the smoke, but by now the creature was slowing to a smouldering stop.

"*Boss?*" Hairy said.

"Small kitchen fire," Taine said. "Under control. Tell the guests to shelter in place."

Scooping up Weiss's rifle, Taine ducked under the smoking mandibles and squeezed a shot up into the creature's mouth, putting it out of its misery.

"Good call," Lefty said, and, his tunic dripping, he leapt off the counter, stalked out into the corridor, and leaned hard on the carving knife that was still protruding from beneath the armoured cuticle, pushing the blade into the creature's brain. The monster quivered.

So, it too had still been alive, the chemical bomb merely paralysing it.

A single antenna swished in the monster's final desperate quest for freedom. The appendage hit the elevator control panel before sinking to the floor.

The elevator rose from the basement, the doors opening to reveal the inside of the empty car.

Hang on...

Still grasping Weiss's rifle, Taine wedged it between the outer doors, holding them open, then leaned in and pushed the button for the fourth floor. The car moved off. Taine waited for it to pass.

"Boss?" Lefty asked.

"Just checking," Taine said.

The elevator car ascending, Taine looked down the shaft expecting to see the crushed carcass of the female.

It was gone.

***

Taine didn't hesitate. Punching the button to bring the car down and prevent the wētā getting back in the hotel, he jumped into the lift shaft.

"McKenna!" Read and Hairy called in unison.

Lefty, though, with his sniper reflexes, didn't miss a beat, jumping a split second after Taine, the two of them dropping just ahead of the descending car.

Taine bent his knees, bracing himself for the impact, still his body shuddered with shock when he landed in the elevator pit. He glanced up; the lift was still dropping.

They'd be no use to anyone trapped in the pit.

Landing, Lefty grunted, letting go the carving knife, which clattered on the concrete beside Taine; the soldier had still been holding it when he leapt, yanking it clear of the wētā in the corridor. It was covered in white goop—wētā brain matter—but oddly there was no blood. Taine scooped up the blade. And thrust it between the outer doors, prising them open.

Above them, the car was still descending.

The angle was wrong. The blade too short.

Taine grunted with effort, levering the elevator doors open, so Lefty could clamber through the gap. Lefty all but dived through, his rifle scraping on the concrete. He didn't slow, simply rolled over, and thrust out a hand to Taine, just as the lift stopped at the first floor.

Taine caught Lefty's eye and gave a quick exhalation of relief.

"Read," Lefty said.

"Remind me to thank him." Clasping Lefty's gloved hand, Taine climbed over the lip. The doors closed behind them. Lying nearby on the concrete was the wētā's severed limb, its hooked barb like a sickle on the concrete.

Where's the rest of it?

Taine gripped the knife and scanned the basement. The wētā was still there, but it had no interest in them. Instead, it was lumbering for the exterior. For freedom. If it got into the community, there would be carnage...

"Hairy! The garage doors," Lefty whispered.

"*Broken,*" Hairy replied. "*We thought it was only the two beasties upstairs, so Gilbert and McNaught blocked the stairs.*"

Taine glanced to his left and saw that the soldiers had rolled a metal dumpster in front of the exit doors and tipped it on its side.

They'd done the job; only no one had counted on this one, the female, still being alive.

The wētā was making for the ramp, its antennae undulating before it, hitting the concrete girders, the metal girders, the ceiling pipes. It was injured. Maybe that made it all the more determined. Perhaps it could taste the forest on the air.

"We have to stop it before it gets outside," Taine said.

"Gilbert and McNaught are bringing a Pinzgauer around," Hairy said.

Lefty looked at Taine, understanding passing between them. Gilbert and McNaught wouldn't make it in time. They were on their own.

"Hey, over here, you fucker!" Lefty shouted.

The wētā barrelled on. Missing a knee, maybe it couldn't hear so well.

Running forward to shelter behind one of the concrete girders, Lefty lifted the Mars-L to his shoulder and opened fire, squeezing off round after round, looking to find a vulnerability between the articulated plates. If only. The shells ricocheted off the insect's armour and still it lumbered for the entrance. Lefty changed tack, blasting at the legs, smashing off a hooked tip and mangling a knee. The sound reverberated in the basement. The wētā didn't stop. Two injured legs, and it barely slowed.

"Lefty! It's not working. We're chasing it out, instead of drawing it in."

"Fuck," Lefty said. He lowered the rifle, but seconds later he raised it again, this time fracturing a ceiling pipe, bringing down a torrent of water.

The wētā stopped, turned, its movement measured and ominous as the water gushed over its black flanks. It hissed.

"Oh shit," said Lefty.

Taine dashed back to the lift and thumped the button. The doors remained firmly closed. He looked up at the panel. What the fuck was the lift doing on the second floor?

Lefty fired again. "Any ideas?" The monster kept coming.

Taine's mind raced. No lift and an upturned dumpster blocking the stairs. Not Taine's first choice for a stand-off. An antenna flew at him and he slashed at it with the knife. This was futile. Like fending off a dragon with a matchstick. The wētā whipped back the appendage, hitting the metal rafters, the girder, then the Tesla.

Wait. The Tesla.

"Lefty, go for the lift."

Still firing, Lefty backed up, hunkering near the girder closest to the lift.

First floor.

Taine dived behind the Tesla. He grabbed the charging cable. Yanked it. But locked into the vehicle's charging port, the cable didn't budge.

Lefty fired again, hitting the monster's compound eye. The beast flinched, wild with fury now. It swung its battered rear leg, the limb smacking the ground just a metre from him. The wētā raked the serrated barbs across the concrete. The antennae swished, hitting the roof, then the girder, looking for anything to vent its rage on.

Basement. The lift pinged and the doors opened.

Lefty's rifle clicked. Empty cartridge.

The wētā lunged, antennae still probing.

Lefty thrust the gun at it.

"Get in the lift!" Taine shouted while the wētā made short work of a picatinny rail. "Go!"

Lefty dived in and hugged the wall to be out of the way of the slapping legs. He turned. Looked at Taine. Hesitated.

"I said, go!"

Lefty punched the button. The doors started to close.

Done crunching through the rifle, the wētā raised its rear leg to slam it down again.

Taine braced his boots on the shiny blue chassis, grasped the cable and yanked like his life depended on it. The muscles of his legs screamed with effort. His hands ached. He grimaced. *Come on!*

At last, the cable broke free, revealing two exposed wires. Taine bounded onto the roof of the Tesla, ready to hurl it at the creature. But the cable was just seven metres long. What if it was too short? Reaching up, Taine touched the cable to the metal girders. Held it there.

The massive leg slammed down on the closed doors.

Lefty was safe, but now Taine was alone.

The creature turned, an antenna snaking through the air, whipping past him, searching.

Wait...

Taine lifted his free hand to the pūrerehua at his chest. Felt for the carved whorls etched into the flattened wood of his instrument. His mentor was gone, but perhaps there was a chance... He closed his eyes, and reached out with his soul for the creature's wairua-spirit. At first, there was nothing, only darkness. But out of the gloom, the creature's spirit spoke, its voice a high-pitched primal keening that seared through Taine's bones. It was a song of heartbreak and agony, of a creature destined to be the last of its kind. Trembling, Taine felt a moment of pity. He was about to respond with his own wairua-spirit, about to relent, when all at once the monster roared, the sound violent and merciless, engulfing Taine in a surge of black rage.

His heart pounding, Taine snapped his eyes open.

The antenna flashed again.

Wait...

The appendage touched the metal girder, the wētā jerking as fifty kilowatts of power pumped through it.

***

When the remains of the wētā, including its desiccating body bag, had been removed to the crematorium, Taine took a moment to call Jules.

She answered immediately. *"Is everyone okay?"* She sounded weary.

"Miller's been hospitalised. Crush injuries. A couple of broken ribs. Your information was helpful, though. Seems even the big ones breathe through their exoskeletons."

She was quiet for a moment. *"I don't suppose you were able to save one."*

"No." Jug hadn't been able to save Johnson either. Commodore Webb was going to have his hands full coming up with a plausible explanation, and not just for the mess in the Geyserland's kitchens.

Jules sighed. *"A new species, and it gets wiped out just like that."*

Taine wanted to say that they weren't exactly talking about a cheeky alpine parrot or an endangered Chesterfield skink here, but as Read had once said, 'If the Defence Force's mission was to save New Zealand lives, Jules's role was to save all its little beasties.'

'How do you justify it?' Jules had asked Taine a lifetime ago, on a tussocked hillside in the Fiordland sounds. 'If someone attacks one of our citizens, they automatically forfeit the right to live, is that it?'

It was simplistic, but yes, that was it. Except, no one had explained that to the wētāpunga, who were just trying to survive. Hell, in a way, it was the same for the coronavirus.

Sometimes, there was no compromise.

"I'm sorry," he said.

There was a pause. *"Hey, I heard on the radio that someone escaped a managed isolation facility using a ladder made of knotted sheets."*

"I heard that, too," Taine said.

END

THE BUBBLE BURSTS

Dustin Dreyling

Tearing down the uneven stretch of asphalt, the twin beams of the Hummer's headlights illuminated the debris in the road. Broken branches, knocked loose by the storm, decorated the short private road to the team's destination like body parts, crunching as such when the vehicle obliterated them.

"Listen up people, here's the rundown," the man in the front passenger's seat spoke to the entire cab. "The facility at the end of this road is owned by Gristox Enterprises. Gristox is owned by Brandon Adams, a rogue geneticist who hooked up with a woman named Samara Mago, one of the heads of Gristox in this region. Mago and her illegal outfit practice black market science of all kinds.

"In this particular instance, we are paying a visit to these less than fine people to secure for our employer, Tamara Oranda, the technology that she has paid for, but has yet to receive. Our soon-to-be, less-than-gracious hosts have not delivered on their end of the bargain after the contractual five years they were given to deliver."

The lone woman in the military vehicle, a mixed-descent giantess with her dark hair pulled back in a bun, spoke next.

"Is this going to be an incapacitate or eliminate mission, *jefe?*" Sharice Gillian asked her boss, Killian Howzer, watching him with eager brown eyes.

The scar-faced, dark-haired man in front turned his head to the side, glancing back at her with his good eye.

"All are expendable."

The grimness in his voice relayed how unenthused he was about ending the lives of the people inside the facility. But a job is a job, and Howzer cared more about their bottom lines than the seedy scientists doing shit they weren't ethically or legally supposed to be. "Fuck 'em!" was his motto when it came to the non-violent criminals they dealt with in their line of work. Unless they were obvious captives, these people knew what they were doing. Culpability was everything.

"Masks," he ordered, drawing up nearer the front gate.

There was some bitching, but nonetheless they donned their face masks. Covid-19 had added an extra annoyance when it came to their field of expertise, two strikes if you included the actual virus itself. Howzer hadn't dealt with it personally, yet. And he intended to keep it that way. He looked at them all, grinning at his choice of masks for his people. He'd spent a small portion of Uncle Sam's budget on some cheesy crap that tickled his nostalgic funny bone. He secured his own mask in place, made up to look like the bottom portion of Jason Voorhees' trademark hockey mask.

Liam Young stopped the Hummer at the gate, then secured his mask before rolling down his window to greet the guard. The man was clearly unimpressed with Young's Hannibal Lecter face covering. Nor did he seem to care for the other horror movie-inspired masks the others wore.

"Identification, please," the guard said. The man's expression betrayed his sense of irritation at having to deal with these people, on a Monday night no less.

Unlike the spec-ops squad, he wore a standard blue disposable face mask. The face diaper made it harder to tell, but the kid looked all of twenty-three, if that. It was doubtful he was anything but a rent-a-cop.

Dammit. I hate collateral damage, Howzer thought right before he took action.

Howzer's right hand swung up from his side, his finger squeezing a fraction of a second later. The bullet exploded from the suppressed barrel of the pistol in his hand, boring into the unprepared fool's forehead, creating a gory blossom. The piece of deadly metal clunked when it ricocheted off the backside of the guard's ridiculous standard-issue helmet.

"Hey—" the other guard in the shack yelled as he scrambled to bring his weapon to bear.

An arrow pierced the man's helmet, blood spurting out around the metallic shaft protruding from between his eyes. A crossbow retracted back inside the rear driver's side window of the Humvee. The door opened and a baseball cap-wearing man jumped out, wearing the lower half of Pennywise's visage in mask form, the nightmare clown-monster's jagged teeth bared and ready to bite.

Stepping into the little guardhouse, Donaldson waved to the camera, his blue eyes twinkling behind his face covering. Without hesitation, he started bashing the surveillance equipment to bits with a pry bar that he seemed to produce from thin air. Donaldson hit the button to open the gate arm, then ripped his arrow out of the skewered security guard's head with an angry yank. He flicked the broadhead at the floor of the shack, most of the blood coating it spattering onto the floor. Then he docked the still wet projectile. Quickly, Donaldson ran back to his seat in the Humvee and shut the door.

"Got any hand sanitizer, guys?" he asked of the group. "Or something to clean the blood off my mitts?"

"Just don't touch your face, jackass," Gutierrez said.

Donaldson looked across the back seat at him. He could see the other man clearly grinning behind his Freddy Krueger mask. His face lined up with the burnt killer's screen-printed grin perfectly. He couldn't help but laugh at the smartass.

"Ain't nobody wants to touch your face, Krueger," Donaldson said.

Gutierrez just laughed.

Young floored it to the front entrance, parking the vehicle. After clearing the entryway of five more guards, they blew through the spacious greeting space and entered the back area. This led down to the meat and potatoes of the building, which included their objective.

Four more guards bought the farm as they made their way down to the laboratory, but so far it had actually been rather easy work for a quiet October evening. Howzer brought them to a set of double doors which in turn led into the primary labs. After peering in and doing a headcount, he looked at everyone behind him and flashed all eight of his fingers. Then with just his right hand he put up only four, as he silently mouthed the meaning behind the gestures.

Eight scientists, four guards.

They all nodded. Message received.

Gutierrez burst in through the doors, his .12 gauge making short work of the first two guards. The Mexican drug smuggler-turned-mercenary cackled like the gangster from *Home Alone* the entire time. Jones stepped up from behind him, his M249 machine gun decimating the panicked scientists behind the guards Gutierrez had just dispatched. Howzer's shotgun roared twice, putting massive holes in the last two guards as they came around the corner of a giant machine.

"I trust we're murdering people for a good reason, yeah, boss man?" Donaldson inquired as they entered the rear of the lab area.

"I hope so, D," Howzer said.

They removed their masks, tucking them away in their pockets. Covid-19 was the least of their worries here. The group advanced, gun barrels pointing in all directions as they scanned the area for enemies. Gutierrez pushed through to the front, shotgun ready, and led the team through a labeled set of doors that corresponded with their destination.

Laboratory.

Inside was an overwhelming array of unrecognizable machinery and computer-controlled equipment. Yellow painted stairs, platforms, and catwalks framed much of the room's interior. These granted access to all parts of each of the monstrous machinations dominating the large lab and workshop. It almost looked more like a factory than a research facility.

At the center of the humming assemblage was a huge, floating sphere. The sphere was an iridescent, ever-changing ball of cool colors, hovering just inches above the floor. As one, the mercs froze in place, transfixed on the otherworldly brain scramble swirling before their eyes.

"Gillian?" Howzer asked. "Would you be a dear, and please enlighten me as to what the devil we are looking at?"

"I dunno, boss man, but this readout suggests these people were into dimensional gateways and whatnot," Howzer's tech expert said, tightening her bun after responding.

"Where is our objective?"

"I'm not sure of that, either…I think it might be in there," Gillian said, glancing at her smart device's readouts again before she pointed at the sphere.

The globular object pulsed concentric circles of red as she extended her index finger in its direction. Like it was aware.

What the hell is inside that thing? Howzer wondered, his blood starting to ice up.

"Gillian, I want you and Young to look around and see if you can figure out what the actual fuck is going on here, or better yet…what *that* is, and what's inside," Howzer pointed at the sphere as he spoke.

The colorful anomaly appeared to respond to his gesture, ripples of red and yellow lingering where his finger would have touched it, had he made physical contact.

"10-4, boss man," Gillian said before she and Young went back to the grouping of desks just inside the entrance to the labs.

"Donaldson and Gutierrez, I want you two to check out the other side of this room. I want to know about any other exits and any more oddball shit like this."

He jerked his thumb in the direction of the sphere, which once again rippled with colors at his extended digit, this time a dark mix of crimson, deep purple, and black.

Like he pissed it off.

"Yessir, boss man," Gutierrez said. He slapped Donaldson as he came up and stood by him. "Hey, Donaldson! Long time no see, *pendejo!*"

"Fuck you," Donaldson said. "You know you missed me, you asshole."

The two men moved off, ribbing each other at a moderate volume and skirting around the equipment surrounding the sphere before they headed toward the other side of the expansive room.

Howzer turned back to look at the sphere and his remaining team members. His breath hitched in his chest as he watched Jones reaching towards the sphere with his exposed finger. The strange object surged with all the colors of the rainbow, all of them concentrated on the place where the stupid man's finger was going to connect with its surface. The sphere's hide or skin or shell or whatever writhed in seeming anticipation, filling Howzer with such intense dread that his heart threatened to attack...

"Jones! Stand down! Do not touch it!" Howzer yelled at the man.

Jones was oblivious, his finger now only a foot away from its exterior. He did not stop, or even acknowledge his commander, a stupid grin on his face beneath vacant eyes.

"I'm on it," Gillian said, Young trailing behind her as they arrived back from their desk search just in time.

She ran at Jones, his finger a mere ten inches away now. Gillian bellowed at him as she closed the short distance. "Get your grubby paws away from it, dumbass!"

Gillian jumped at him, trying to close the distance faster than she could run. She succeeded, colliding with the smaller Jones. The sound that escaped him on impact briefly reminded her of the cartoons she watched as a kid on Saturday mornings.

"*Yipe!*" he shouted as she took him down, his pinky finger grazing the side of the sphere as they both fell to the floor, the digit slicing a visible gash across its outer layer.

Howzer could not properly comprehend the color of the electricity that surged and crackled all over the surface of the object. Its round surface bubbled and spasmed like a covered pot of boiling water left on the burner for too long. The smells of ozone, electricity, and something... *unknown* permeated the air with a palpable thickness. As if to accentuate the mysterious smell, a form pushed out on the exterior of the sphere. Before anyone watching's mind could fathom *what* they were seeing, the bubble burst.

With a deep popping sound, the sphere disintegrated into phantasmagorical pieces that shimmered from existence before their eyes. In the color-changing object's place, a collection of otherworldly madness remained. A pile of strange, alien lifeforms writhed like a snake orgy as things not of Earth untangled themselves from one another. All kinds of freakish appendages twisted and flailed about as things from a different dimension tasted the air in the world of humans for what was likely the first time.

Howzer's mind tried to devour itself as he stared at the things the sphere had shit into existence; his team stunned by the things they were looking at. They were the kind of hideous things that you couldn't *un*see.

As if the collective of horror suddenly got its shit together, the pile of lifeforms spread out into the labs as well as the hallway beyond before anyone could react. Slithering things, flying terrors, and stalking abominations fled the armed mercenaries, who finally realized they had firearms sitting lifeless in their hands.

"Open fire!" Howzer yelled.

Their weapons all came alive at once, tearing into the bulk of the twisting, squirming, skittering creatures. Monsters with too many legs, not enough legs, and no legs at all went down. Howzer's team would still have to work to get out of this one alive.

A disturbing creature that looked like a cross between a xenomorph facehugger and a mayfly flew at Howzer. He brought his shotgun around and blasted the thing out of the air just before it had landed on his head. It blew apart into a hundred gory pieces, much of which coated Howzer.

For a split second, he legitimately worried that the thing's blood was going to start to eat his flesh like the movie monster's acidic vitae. When the burning didn't come, he concentrated on the other things once more, blasting a similar animal out of the sky as it zig-zagged across the open space above his head. It whimpered like a kicked dog, crashing to the floor hard and leaving a gory pink trail behind its body.

Without missing a beat, Howzer spun around and fired at some kind of tentacled rabbit-looking critter. It jumped six feet in the air and covered just as much distance in his direction with each hop. His shotgun clicked empty, and he swore, no time to reload. Howzer's pistol refused to come out of its holster as he tried to draw on the psychotic rodent from where-the-hell-ever.

"Dammit!" he shouted, out of time.

The octo-bunny sunk its sharp incisors into his neck. Howzer's lifeblood gushed from the gaping tear in his flesh, the thing repeatedly stabbing him with three-inch serrated choppers. It purred at him as it bit into his neck again and again, the man flailing uselessly as consciousness slipped away from him. His pistol, finally free of the holster, clattered to the floor next to his discarded .12 gauge. All the while, he grabbed feebly at the fluffy creature killing him.

Its furry tentacles wrapped around his neck and hands, ensuring he would not be able to remove it from his neck before dying. Howzer was sure he heard the purr turn into guttural sounds that could only be laughter. It was chuckling at his demise.

"F-f-fugggck...you!" Howzer managed to growl before he bit down on the rabbit-thing's head, an easy feat, since its plush fur was practically in his mouth, anyway.

It squealed like the Earth equivalent—an ear-shredding shriek that still sounded innocent enough to cause a pang of regret inside Howzer as its rotten blood filled his mouth. Gagging, bile surged up his throat to help expel the nasty life fluids from his word hole. The bloody puke soaked the attacking animal, which responded with revulsion. The octo-rabbit let loose with a cry of distress at the added insult to its injury, then bounced away from him.

"Howzer!" Gillian shouted over the gunfire in the room, managing to reach the dying man's ears.

She ran towards him, dodging about a dozen different things from a dozen different nightmares. A three-headed thing that looked like some kind of scorpion-dog-dinosaur almost snagged her with its synchronized canine jaws sat atop serpentine necks. Gillian just managed to avoid the snapping teeth and stabbing scorpion tail, the last complete with a venomous stinger.

As she sidestepped the triple attack, Gillian spun around in a way that presented her with a shot at the monster's backside. Her right arm came up, her Uzi unleashing a 9mm bullet storm into the tricephalic thing—right where its three necks came together. It screamed. Not a roar, or a screech, or wild animal bellow. It *screamed.* Like a scared little child.

She felt instantly sick, her mind knowing better but her sudatory senses still convinced she had just shot up a little kid. A *human.* Ignoring the foolish side of her brain, she continued firing into the thing until it dropped in a pool of reddish-brown ichor.

"Go to hell, you sad ass wannabe Monster Zero," Gillian said.

Her face flushed with embarrassment at her lame one-liner, so she fired twice more into it, until the weapon clicked on an empty chamber. In a flash, she swapped magazines while running to Howzer's side. Dropping down beside him, she tried to staunch the blood flowing out of his neck the best she could with her meagre medical supplies. The gauze quickly turned red, but she seemed to have lessened the flow. It didn't look good for her boss.

***

Gutierrez and Young were cornered. After the sphere burst, they were discovered by alien worms in the space of about twenty seconds. Huge ones, four feet long, possessing centipede legs and nasty jaws like a Bobbit worm. The two men were backed into a surgical space in the corner, with a half-dozen of the giant, annelid-like things surrounding them. Worse, Gutierrez's shotgun had jammed on him, and he was desperately trying to fix it and fire his sidearm at the same time.

Young, on the other hand, aimed at the closest worm with his Barry Burton Special revolver. The creature swayed back and forth like a cobra. He fired the .44 Magnum blowing the thing's head apart. Another worm latched onto his forearm before he could react, the lancing pain from the wicked jaws causing Young to drop his weapon.

It climbed up his bicep to his head and shoulders. The vile lifeform wrapped itself around his neck and face, choking him with the rancid coating of goo covering its hot skin. Like some jelly-slathered constrictor, the worm was grinding on his face in an attempt to smother him. It wasn't long before Young started feeling dreamy, and even though he knew it was likely because his brain needed fresh oxygen, it was more than that. It felt...*good*. Too good.

Young began to giggle, the laughter muffled inside the coils. He was somewhere else, a different place made of darkness, but there was no pain. No fear. No monsters trying to kill him. Just the one trying to fuck his face. *I'm high, this slimy shit is making me loopy,* the thought breaking through the fog covering his mind.

With a muffled howl of anger, he tore at the nasty thing wrapped around his head, just as its lengthy serrated mandibles bit into the back of his neck. Young wailed, locked in the worm's grip. His body dropped to the floor and started to convulse. Blood gushed all around the worm's buried head, its jaws wreaking havoc on the nerves going from the poor man's brain to the rest of his body. As a result, Young's limbs flopped around like they were made of rubber as he seized and spasmed on the gore-slicked tile floor.

With a final chomp, it severed his head. Young's top piece squeezed out from the worm's coils like a turd, tumbling to the floor with an inaudible *splaaat!* His body fell, the worm with it. Once on the floor, it skittered away on dozens of legs, fleeing Gutierrez's screaming vengeance.

His weapon fully functional once more, Gutierrez went to work.

The semi-automatic shotgun barked flame as he blasted Young's killer. It blew apart in a splash of green blood and red innards. His next round of quick succession shots eradicated the next few nasties behind it. Frightened off by this, the last two worms beat a hasty retreat, slithering up a yellow railing before disappearing into one of the unknown machines decorating the laboratory. Gutierrez followed up the small flight of yellow-painted steel steps and searched the towering contraption's guts.

Mysterious electronic components surrounded by circuit boards and wires filled the majority of internal space inside whatever the hell kind of machine it was. Gutierrez spotted a trail of slime that went under what looked to be a cooling unit or something similar, given the fan connected to it. The electrical server smell combined with the ooze the worms secreted created a rank odor so bad he doubled over and began puking uncontrollably.

Gutierrez saw something big approaching from his periphery while he vomited, his shotgun coming up fast and belching flame as he continued to hurl. Neither blast had much of an effect on the new foe, as he was promptly knocked aside like a rag doll. He looked up at the thing towering over him. It's head appeared to be made of leeches, a hundred wriggling, reaching bodies stretching to caress his face.

He backpedaled, falling to the vomit-covered catwalk and scooting back from the hideous form creeping towards him. Its legs seemed to lack an internal skeleton, the multitude of limbs bending impossibly at different angles as it pulled itself along the steel grating.

From what seemed like very far away, he could hear Gillian. She was shouting Howzer's name and telling him to hold on, while Jones screamed somewhere beyond her. Donaldson yelled in between the blasts of his weapon, the closest of the team to him. The monster was nearly upon Gutierrez now, his teammates the least of his concerns.

Gutierrez struggled to get back on his feet, his shotgun feeling like it weighed a hundred pounds in his hands. Digging deep to find his strength, he was able to scoop it up from the grate quickly. His combat shotgun barked once again, the slug streaking out of it and connecting with his enemy in a big way. The leech-head monster blew apart at the torso, its main body exploding in a spray of what looked like antifreeze but smelled like a wrestler's sweaty ass mixed with puke and blood. Getting weak from his injuries, the kickback knocked Gutierrez off his feet. The timing could not have been better, as something streaked through the airspace where his head had been a second prior and slammed into the machine behind him with a brutal *cruuunch!*

Sparks flew everywhere, singeing Gutierrez on the floor below. He looked up at a confusing blade of an appendage, embedded in the metal shell behind his head and connected to its owner by a dripping, ropy tendril of an arm. The stinky secretions covering it dripped onto his leg, and he braced for the agony of it eating into his flesh. Instead, the rank odor of it caused him to dry heave, his stomach already empty of its contents long before.

"*Dios mio,* you *pedazos de mierda* fucking *stink,*" he spat at the thing that would have skewered him.

It was one big mouth on legs, with two frog eyes situated at the top of its head. The fucking thing looked ridiculous, and Gutierrez felt a flash of shame at probably getting killed by such an illogical being. Like some creator's lame-ass attempt to make Pac-man a real creature. Except the famous video game icon didn't have a tongue like this asshole.

The blade tongue tore itself out of the machine with a whipping motion, smoke and sparks spurting from the damaged machine. Gutierrez was burned again, this time by white-hot particles as they rained down on him from the gash rent in the big piece of machinery.

A booming roar preceded the monster's insides exploding out through its overlarge mouth. Pieces of its tongue, uvula, and throat covered the floor along with its orange blood. It made a croaking noise like a frog before collapsing to the floor. Gutierrez looked up at Gillian standing where the monster had been a second prior, reloading her smoking weapon. She was drenched in several shades of blood, a look of solemn rage etched into her face.

"Howzer?" Gutierrez asked, knowing the answer before he asked it.

She shook her head, a single tear threatening to spill down her face.

"Jones? Donaldson?"

"Donaldson is looking for the object. Jones is bleeding out from an attack by some freaky mantis thing that severed his femoral. I can't stop the blood flow. He's as good as dead."

Gutierrez suddenly realized something.

"Where the hell did they all go?" he asked, aware of both the silence and lack of movement in the room.

"I don't know. Whatever we haven't killed just up and fled, all at once," Gillian said, nervously glancing around. "I just hope they weren't running *from* something."

"What the hell could they be running from?"

"I don't know, but I sure don't want to find out," she said. "Let's get the fuck out of here, yeah? While some of us are still alive." She helped him up, Gutierrez grunting in pain as he was forced to put weight on his left leg.

They walked through a sea of gore. Dead alien things covered the ground, most in shredded pieces. They came upon Young's headless corpse, Gillian pulling the Burton special from his dead fingers. She checked the chambers, then patted his corpse down for more ammo. Finding some, she reloaded the Python revolver while a limping Gutierrez covered her.

"How are you on slugs?" she asked.

"There's two left in here and six more in my side pocket," he answered. Then, as an afterthought, he filled the chamber up with slugs. "I need to get the rest of Howzer's shells."

Gillian nodded. "He's over there…by Jones."

They made their way over to the other section where the sphere had been. Howzer's and Jones' corpses lay a mere ten feet from each other, close to a bank of computer monitors. Gillian picked up Jones' machine gun. She checked the magazine drum and clipped it back into place before nodding at Gutierrez.

He emptied Howzer's weapon, adding the expelled slugs to his chest bandolier. In the distance, something chattered, the shrill staccato sounding like some kind of psycho squirrel with a mouthful of phlegm. In response, another something shrieked. A freakish sound, reminiscent of a bird. Both sounded far away, in a different room perhaps.

"Where are they going?" he asked.

"Out. Where else?" was all she said in reply.

Gutierrez finished pillaging Howzer's ammo, taking a second to say a prayer for the man under his breath.

"Quit with the religious shit, let's get the hell out of here," Gillian said.

"We need to find the objective," Gutierrez reminded her. "We need to give some sort of meaning to their deaths, no?"

Gillian nodded. "Hopefully, Donaldson found it already."

***

Donaldson had not found the item they were all dying for. Instead, he had found the worst of the beings previously contained by the sphere. It was a grower, not a shower. At some point he had exited the lab, continuing down the hall to another room marked 'specimen storage.' Inside, he found hundreds of specimen jars sitting on rack upon rack of display shelving. All manner of things were kept inside the jars, from animals to human fetuses to body parts from multiple organisms.

Just looking at them turned Donaldson's stomach. Donaldson was never one to get nauseated, so the fact he was sick to his stomach threw him off a little. He meandered amongst the shelves, keeping an eye out for anything that looked more important than dead tissue in formaldehyde.

With his MK17 out in front of him, he carefully walked past the seemingly endless rows of specimens, glancing in each direction before continuing. He could see space open up after the shelves ended on the other side of the long, corridor-like warehouse area. He smelled the blood before he saw the drying pool of it on the floor beyond the racks of jars.

"Great," he mumbled to himself, the whisper seeming as loud as a shout in the quiet room.

With a rumbling boom, a generator somewhere in the back flared to life, scaring the shit out of him. The floor vibrated as he made his way towards the sound, weapon up and ready. When he reached the end of the specimen shelves, he could see the trap doors past the dried pool of blood on the floor opening up, revealing the ceiling of what could only be a cage set into the floor. Before Donaldson's brain was able to properly process just what he was seeing, the top of the floor cage lifted up, flying open on ruined pneumatic hinges.

Something in the cage screamed like a tyrannosaurus being skinned alive.

"Aww, fuck me in the goat ass," he said, backing towards the entrance he had just come through.

Gnarled claws with swollen knuckles reached up and grasped the raised edges of the floor above the enclosure. Demonic talons sank into the retracted linoleum-covered panels that normally hid the cage. A grunting form pulled itself up with two immense, muscular arms covered in severe burns. Donaldson pissed himself as its head rose out of the hole and looked at him hungrily.

A long, scaled snout greeted him, narrow and tapering like a crocodile. The muzzle itself looked more like that of a feline, with whiskered lips that covered vicious fangs. The whiskers moved independently of each other, squiggling like worms on the thing's face. At the back end of its head sat a pair of glowing red eyes, punctuated in the middle with bright white pupils. They glared at Donaldson.

He opened fire on the beast as it pulled itself out of its prison, punching holes into its emerging form with his rifle. It growled as bloody wounds exploded all over its reptilian flesh, but the firepower did nothing to deter it from climbing free from the concealed oubliette in the floor. Rising to its full height—Donaldson backing the hell up as it did so—it stretched and cracked its knuckles, as a human would upon waking. It was ten feet tall, easy, and decidedly humanoid. Crocodilian scales covered most of its flesh, marred slightly in the places he had shot it.

He quit wasting his ammo, the lack of effect it had on this new monster deterring him from even continuing. That and he was scared out of his mind. Donaldson hoped the others would catch up soon, or he was screwed. The thing's jaws split wide open, the skinned tyrannosaur cry shredding his ears with a blast of sound that shook him to his core. It smelled worse than a dead animal in an Arizona outhouse in the middle of an August day. Donaldson joined Gutierrez at the puke party by dropping to his knees and throwing up all over the floor. Still, he recovered quickly, rising and firing three short bursts of his MK17. The creature yelled in pain, its voice very human in a disturbing way.

"What the hell are you supposed to be, anyway?" he asked nobody as he opened fire once more.

The monster twitched a little as new bullet holes opened across its body, but the beast did not stop. Donaldson had had enough of its shit. He flipped the thing off and ran for the door. It gave chase, the monster's pounding feet causing him to turn back and look. His guts seemed to rebel against him when he saw it closing the distance between them with drooling jaws agape. A deadly tongue dangled out the corner of its mouth, its serrated-looking surface quivering in anticipation.

Donaldson ran out into the hall connecting the lab areas. Gillian and Gutierrez were there, running toward him. He waved them back.

"Not this way! Big...big bear..." he panted as he ran in their direction. "Big bear...chase me!"

The wall behind him exploded as a massive being tore through it like it was cardboard. Dust billowed up into the air and quickly filled the corridor. The monster turned and charged through the cloud at them, its drooling tongue waving behind it cartoonishly from the corner of its mouth. The three legs it stood on were somehow working together to propel it forward in a gallop, with both arms raised above its head to attack. A second mouth opened in its stomach, splitting the gut between two pairs of abdominal muscles. A thick black tongue shot out, nearly catching his foot before snapping back.

"Oh fuck!" Gillian shouted, blasting the new orifice with her Uzi.

The fusillade cut the monstrosity off right as it started to roar from its original head, the neutered noise sounding like a nervous gulp from one of the Three Stooges. Brackish maroon liquid seeped from the toothy opening in its belly, and the black tongue licked its stomach muscle lips, smearing the dark blood all over. Slavering crocodilian jaws opened wide as it came bouncing, imitating Tigger from *Winnie the Pooh.*

Gutierrez pulled out his knife and threw it at the jumping beast, hoping like hell his skills had held up over time. He was rewarded with a meaty *thunk!* as the blade impaled the creature in what they thought was its chest. It crashed hard to the floor, instantly going still. Silence reigned for several moments, each of them unsure what to do. Then steeling himself, Gutierrez cautiously approached the downed enemy, his shotgun trained on it the whole time. Donaldson followed with his MK, and Gillian trailed with her weapon covering their six.

"So, did you find the object?" Gillian asked Donaldson. "Or did we waste our time coming to save you?"

Donaldson grinned, batting his eyes at the larger woman. "*Ma Cherie*, I did not know that you cared!"

"You wish, needle-dick," she said.

Gutierrez slapped Donaldson's arm. Donaldson gave him a questioning look.

"What?" he asked, incredulous.

"Don't be stupid. Answer the lady," Gutierrez said. "Did. You. Find. The fucking object?"

Donaldson cracked a grin and nodded his head sheepishly. "Ayuh. You betcha, Mr. Gonzalez, I sure did."

His impression of the Loony Toons buzzard was spot on.

"What did I tell you about calling me that?" Gutierrez said, looking back over his shoulder at the downed monster.

It was still prone, motionless...save for the slight rise and fall of its chest.

"*El hijo de puta!*" he yelled, proceeding to blast the horrid thing some more.

Gore covered the walls and ceiling along with the floor. The fluorescent light above was muted by the spatter. Gutierrez shot the corpse up until he clicked empty, now down to the slugs in his bandolier. Still, the beast did not move, effectively minced meat.

They moved to the door leading back to the complex's entrance. Before heading back through, Gillian stopped Donaldson with a hand to his chest. "Give it."

Donaldson laughed and handed her a Rubik's cube-sized box, a lock adorning one side, with a pair of hinges on the opposite edge. It was even colored similar to the 1980's analog game device. Sectioned off into squares, each had a different color than any of the other squares around it, and each colored square had a unique character of what was likely Japanese. This was according to Donaldson, who was a self-professed lover of the Pacific Island nation and thought himself an expert based on all of the manga, anime, and films he sought out to fill his free time. Nobody cared enough to argue with his assessment, so they continued towards the entrance.

Stepping carefully around the sticky mess that was the deceased monster, they made it through the door without incident, the trio fairly confident that their foe was indeed dead. Gutierrez pushed through the double doors at the end, leading them into the corridor that would take them back outside. The halls were silent as a tomb, their footfalls the only sounds. Donaldson started humming *I Think We're Alone Now*, receiving swift looks of death from his remaining companions.

"Okay, sorry," he held his hands up in surrender, the scene going silent once more.

"What I wanna know," Gillian spoke up suddenly, making Donaldson jump, "is where the hell those things came from."

Donaldson laughed, suddenly whirling around to look behind them before explaining himself. "It doesn't matter, does it? Those weren't exactly Earth lifeforms, that's all we need to know," he said. "And I don't even want to know that much! We lost half our team tonight, including Howzer! What the shit are we going to do now?"

"Let's get the fuck out of here and get our prize money first, Terry, then we'll worry about crossing that bridge," Gillian said solemnly, her sadness over their losses threatening to consume the woman.

"What we *should* be asking ourselves," Gutierrez began, "is where the hell did all of those things go? There is no way we killed them all!"

The trio walked out into the entryway, their Hummer visible through the front windows. Glass covered the floor of the lobby, remnants from the broken panes that stretched from wall to wall. It was obvious some of the missing critters had moseyed on through this way. Donaldson spied a lone worm slithering towards the trees at the edge of the facility parking lot. He pointed at it until both companions saw it as well, then smacked his head in dismay.

"What?" Gillian asked.

"I don't suppose either of you thought to grab the keys from Liam?" he asked.

The jingling sound Donaldson was hoping to hear brought their attention to the keys dangling from Gutierrez's fingers. "Right here, *pendejo.*"

"Excellent!" he cried out and snatched the keyring from Gutierrez.

Behind them, a rumble began to swell. It was coming from inside the building. Donaldson hurried to the driver's side door and unlocked it, instantly repeating the process for the rest of the doors with the button once he got it open. They felt a surge of static electricity wash over them, arcs of it surging between the hapless mercs and the metal frame of their ride. All three yelped as they received a jolt that made their fillings rattle and assholes pucker.

"Can we get the fuck out of here, please?" Donaldson asked in a pathetic voice.

"Get in, you baby. It's just a little electrical surge, I'm sure it only means the building is going to explode," Gillian said, laughing.

"Let's not stick around to see if you're right, okay?" Gutierrez said, pointing out the way they came in. *"Vámonos, cabrón!"*

Donaldson floored it, the Hummer screeching into motion. They cruised back down the drive, blowing past the guard shack. If anything from the sphere had escaped the facility, it did not go this way. The ground beneath them rolled, tossing the truck to one side of the drive, which remained blissfully upright. A millisecond later they were assaulted by a crackling electric boom that stunned them silly. Donaldson hit the brakes and threw the vehicle into Park before looking back.

"Oh shit."

"No shit," Gutierrez said, also looking back.

"What the fu—" Gillian began, but stopped short when she too looked behind them.

Where they had come from, the facility full of dead bodies—three of their own included—had been replaced by an undulating sphere of electrical current, roiling and pulsing in a ball of energy where a building had once been. The smell of it permeated the air inside the vehicle, even as many yards away as they were. Whatever technology had been inside Gristox Labs was lost to the shambling dimensional gateway that seemed to be…growing?

"Oh hell, get us the *fuck* out of here—*pronto!*" Gutierrez cried out, realizing how bad they had likely fucked up…

…unless their coveted prize could stop an expanding dimensional gateway to a plane of existence filled with monstrous aberrations. That was assuming, of course, that their employer desired such an outcome. For all they knew, she had wanted this to happen. The head of Oranda Enterprises, Incorporated was very much a loose cannon. For all Howzer had known, Tamara wanted nothing more than to bring about the end of the world this way. Or not.

Donaldson sped off in the direction of their rendezvous point in Minneapolis. He looked in the rearview mirror at the sky and horizon behind them. It had taken on a crackling bluish hue that glowed in the early morning light. A color he watched expand before they drove over a hill. Just before he was about to look back to the road in front of him, a shape in the rearview mirror caught his eyes. It was no more than a silhouette, moving on the horizon, following them, and keeping up.

It had three legs.

END

THE APOCALYPSE DRIVE

Justin Coates

Our world has passed away,
In wantonness o'erthrown.
There is nothing left to-day
But steel, and fire, and stone.

- Rudyard Kipling, *"For All We Have and Are"*

The M1 Gideon super-tank, *Behold the Behemoth,* plowed through the ruins of Virginia. It was raining ashes. PSICOM officer Captain Kelly Andrada watched the gray sheets falling through her periscope. The sky was dying, shedding its necrotic flesh in vast flurries of grey particulate. The sun fared little better, smoke from a hundred burning cities reducing it to a dull orb.

From his seat just below her, Private Amir skillfully maneuvered them through the wreckage on the freeway. There weren't many things that could stop the *Behemoth*: whatever Amir couldn't drive around, he drove over. Hull mounted thermal and infrared cameras allowed them to keep going even when the ashfall reduced visibility.

"If we keep this up, we'll reach Arlington in half an hour," she said, her microphone carrying her words to the headsets of twenty crew members stationed at various points throughout the massive war machine. "Last-minute combat checks on all systems. We're going in shooting."

Her adjutant, Major Lasky, glanced up from his computer station below. "Ma'am, Dragon 6 wants a situation report on Exalted Fiddler's movement before then."

"Tell General Townsend that Fiddler hasn't changed positions," Andrada replied. She could *feel* the monster lurking like a trapdoor spider in the swirling hell of the noosphere. "Still in the aether just below our plane. It's too close to the surface to turn back. It *will* breach at Arlington."

Lasky nodded and fired off a secured message.

General Townsend would take her word for it. He'd accepted her command recommendation from PSICOM for a reason. Andrada was the only one to have encountered the demi-god and lived to tell of it. *We're tied together, me and thee,* the psychic officer thought, remembering the night it killed the two hundred souls of her armored company.

The generals and the politicians sitting in the relocated capital of Phoenix, Arizona, still didn't fully understand the enemy. Not even PSICOM did, despite knowing more than anyone else. The monsters that had emerged from a hundred-thousand warp gates across the planet three years prior weren't invading for water or material resources. As far as PSICOM could tell, they didn't even need to eat (though they devoured every living thing in their path). Whatever they truly wanted was as unfathomable as the dreadful gods whose idols they erected over the scorched remains of human cities.

Exalted Fiddler was one of those gods, though in the barely decipherable tongue of the enemy, they called it "Ubolzhach." Andrada switched radio channels and addressed the armored convoy racing to reinforce the beleaguered defenders of Arlington.

"All elements, this is Ironside Actual. ETA to contact 30 mikes. Let's not keep the squids waiting. Ironside out."

***

"There's another push coming soon," Sergeant Norris said when she slid back into the trench. "I can feel it."

Private Aaron Temple looked up from the ceaseless task of cleaning the ash from his rifle. The haphazardly piled corpses that lined the blood-soaked earth shifted as he got to his feet. Their section of the trench, Echo Line, was at the top of a shallow hill, one of ten fortifications that formed a massive defensive position curving North along the Potomac river. The radioactive ruins of Washington D.C. still burned from the fury of the enemy advance on the other side of the waterway.

"We hurt 'em bad over the last few days," Norris said, adjusting her shotgun bandolier. She set her jaw, stretching old scars; a legacy from the fall of Baltimore. "They're gonna give this next one all they got."

"No. 3 Corps will be here before then," Lieutenant Burley replied. He didn't sound convinced. None of them were.

"That's what we heard three days ago. We're not going to survive the next push when it comes." Cantu said what they were all thinking, the machine gunner's derisive laugh startlingly loud in the depths of the trench.

"Maybe not," Norris replied. "But we'll damn sure hold the line."

"With what, Sarn't? We're down to a few hundred rounds. Every unit in Echo Line is running low." Cantu pointed to Private Ericks, their radio operator and artillery observer. "Is Ericks gonna hit them with his hand mic? What are we gonna hold the line with when we're outta ammo?"

"With bayonets and our goddamn teeth if we have to," Norris said. "These squid bastards don't get to have Arlington. Not while we're still breathin'." She turned to Burley. "Sir, I suggest we disregard the water rationing order. We're not gonna get another chance to hydrate before Squidward comes calling."

Temple wiped the ashes from his gas mask lenses. *Before they overrun us, you mean. Before they skin us alive and drag us back into whatever Hell they came from.*

"Right," the lieutenant said. "Uh...yes. Good idea, Sergeant. Everyone drink what you've got."

Temple pulled a canteen from his hip and attached the straw to his mask's hydration port. There was barely a sip of tepid water left, a few drops falling from a shrapnel hole in the side of the canteen. His heart sank.

"I'm black on water," he said aloud.

None of the other survivors responded at first. Then Cantu laughed. "Go fuck yourself, Temple."

"Enough," Norris snapped, retrieving her own canteen. "I got extra."

"Don't, Sarn't. Temple doesn't deserve shit from us."

"I said *enough,* Specialist. Bad enough we gotta fight Squidward. No reason to fight each other too."

Norris handed Temple her canteen without looking at him. That hurt him more than Cantu's insults.

You deserve worse. Worse than they know.

The sharp blast of outgoing artillery snapped their attention to the front. Ericks' radio crackled. The RTO put the hand mic to his ear, repeating the voice coming over the net.

"All elements, this is Tango HQ," he said, the indirect rounds screaming in overhead. "ISR assets confirm enemy units inbound. Standby to deny enemy assault."

"Oh, shit," Burley whispered. "They're...uh, they're..."

"They're making a push!" Norris shouted. "Get in position!"

Temple stowed the canteen on his kit and snatched up his M4A1. He took a breath to calm himself before clambering up the short wooden ladder to the battlements.

Squid artillery began counter-firing. Huge bursts of superheated gas arched into the air. The horizon briefly filled with fire before the rounds impacted across the trench in a splash of lethal plasma. Men burned alive. Many were thrown from the battlements, joining the growing piles of corpses below. The smell of cooking flesh mingled with the sickly-sweet smell of decomposition.

It reminded Temple of how Benjamin died. He tried desperately not to think of it. He pulled his rifle snug into his shoulder. Beads of sweat stung his eyes. He aimed his rifle at the enemy perimeter barely a kilometer away. The squid hid their army behind a wall of coral-like material secreted by gigantic, stinking polyps.

Norris called it out as she watched through her binoculars. "Alright, here they come!"

A wave of Voidborn clones and bleating N'nogug bioweapons swarmed out of the hive, heading toward them. Temple waited, not wanting to waste precious ammunition until the enemy was closer. *These aren't aliens,* he thought, not for the first time. *These are demons.* His bowels shifted. He prayed he wouldn't shit himself again.

The heavy guns of the 1/40th were already in range. MK-19 grenade launchers and M2 .50 caliber machine guns belched their deadly projectiles into the onrushing horde from concrete pillboxes spread across the battlements. M240-L 7.62mm machine guns chattered among the booming voices of the larger guns. Behind Echo Line, from the relative safety of Tango HQ, artillery and mortar batteries continued their punishing barrage. Observers like Ericks shouted orders through their radios, swiftly adjusting the trajectory of the indirect fire weapons.

Temple exhaled, then squeezed the trigger at the very bottom of his breath. The 5.56mm tungsten round, its flanks etched with psycho-reactive runes, punched out the back of a clone's soft skull. Temple fired again. The bullet glanced off a N'nogug, sending chunks of black ooze flying from the creature's slug-like body. He kept a grisly tally in his mind with each kill. Through his combat scope, the targets grew larger.

The wall of fire coming at the swarm did not deter the aliens. Thousands more poured from behind the coral reef, attacking every section of the trench at once.

"Bayonets!" Sergeant Norris shouted. "Squid stickers and hold, men!"

Temple drew his yatagan bayonet from its sheath. Twenty inches of cold steel burned in the light of the runes covering its polished surface. He snapped the blade into place and rose to a crouch behind the sandbag battlements.

The enemy reached the razor-wire perimeter two hundred meters away. The few remaining claymore anti-personnel mines detonated in clouds of ash and dust. The aliens rushed over their fallen kin without slowing. Temple switched to controlled pairs, putting two rounds into each target before shifting fire.

Cantu fired on cyclic beside him. His M249 Squad Automatic Weapon (SAW) cleared a bloody half-circle in the shrieking mob clawing their way up the hill. Ericks stowed his radio in his assault pack and fought with his pistol, firing single shots whenever Sergeant Norris paused to reload her shotgun. The lieutenant shivered, crouched behind the battlements with his hands pressed to the sides of his head.

The machine guns and artillery fell silent at almost the same time. After three days of near constant battle, their ammunition was finally spent.

"I'm black on ammo," Cantu said a moment later. He ditched his heavy automatic rifle on the ground and drew his yatagan like a short sword.

A nearby explosion of enemy plasma made Lieutenant Burley yelp. He lurched to his feet and disappeared back into the trench. Cantu snatched up his rifle and equipped his bayonet.

The enemy closed the last few meters, howling nothingness in the clones' glittering compound eyes.

"For the dead of Arlington!" Norris shouted. "Victory, by force and valor!"

"By force and valor!" Temple shouted out the squadron battle cry with the rest of Echo Line as the alien charge hit home.

A gibbering alien clone ran chest first into Temple's bayonet. The arcane symbols on the blade blew its eyes out of its head. Gore sprayed over Temple's gas mask. His arms ached from the impact. He kicked the dead alien backward into its wretched kin. Temple drew back his rifle and hacked off a squid's writhing tentacle. The blood fogged his lenses. He swung, blinded, feeling his yatagan carve through rubbery flesh. Sweat stung his eyes. He blinked furiously, breath coming in ragged gasps of hot, stinking air.

The aliens fired their short-range microwave guns. The wire-covered weapons boiled their screaming victims to death from the inside with a hiss of superheated fluid. One of the soldiers next to Temple popped like a blister.

Cantu sang a cadence as he fought. "All is fair, but you can't compare to the airborne infantry!"

Temple could just make out the words over the din of two hundred troopers battling desperately to hold the line.

Cantu swung his rifle like a glaive, hip-firing on automatic whenever there was a lull in the foe's advance. "Kill, kill, kill! With a cold blue steel!"

A squid clone's tentacles slithered around Temple's left arm. He took aim with his free hand and squeezed the trigger. The gun clicked. *Empty.*

The squid's other limbs wrapped around him. It hissed and squealed, struggling to bring its microwave gun to bear. Warmth spread down Temple's legs. He'd pissed himself.

Make it quick, you bastard. Come on. Do it.

Another paratrooper lunged in, driving a bayonet into the squid's guts. The alien shrieked and burst into flames. It released Temple, toppling backward.

Temple turned, breathless with terror. A dead man stood beside him. His rescuer was a corpse, flesh blackened by hellfire. A bloody exit wound blossomed where its left eye should have been.

Temple knew that wound. He'd been the only one willing to give it, and the rest of his team had never forgiven him.

"The one they call Ubolzhach is coming," the ghost said. Its voice was a rattling wheeze through a gas mask that dripped with blood. "The dead follow in his wake."

It pointed a skeletal finger over Temple's shoulder. He whipped around in time to see a N'nogug lurching toward him. Temple leaped back into nothingness. He fell, and the N'nogug fell with him.

Getting his yatagan upright saved his life. The bayonet burst from the N'nogug's back as it landed squarely on his chest. All the air rushed from Temple's lungs. The creature thrashed wildly, the blade's runes burning it up from the inside.

Other troopers, not seeing him, rushed in to finish the N'nogug off. They stamped him deeper between the corpses. Temple gasped for air as the blood-soaked mud of the trenches swallowed him alive.

A strong hand gripped him by the back of the uniform and pulled him upward, but his gas mask caught on the exposed bones of a vivisected trooper. He pulled it free. He sucked in a lungful of stinking muck that made him vomit down the front of his uniform.

Sergeant Norris stood over him. "Come on, you!" The veteran hacked a clone to pieces with her bayonet. The sacred icons on the shotgun blade glowed a brilliant shade of blue. Norris took a step back, pumped her shotgun, and blasted another alien in half.

She turned to Temple, her eyes alight as she offered her hand. "On your feet, private! No time for shut-eye!"

Norris hauled him up just as a massive N'nogug tumbled from the battlements behind her. The roaring alien bio-weapon showered them with half-digested body parts.

The sergeant pivoted. She put two shells into it before its writhing pseudopods wrapped around her. Norris screamed as it hoisted her into the air. Without a second thought, the monster ripped her in half, throwing her torso aside and shoving her legs down its maw.

Temple stumbled forward. Blood (*Norris' blood, god have mercy, it's Norris' blood*) rained onto him. He rammed his bayonet into the N'nogug. Soldiers piled in with their own melee weapons. Temple wrenched his bayonet out and drove it back in. He ducked, screaming Norris' name, as its death throes crushed two more troopers to death.

Norris' upper torso lay a few feet away. A wounded clone crouched on her chest, a beaked mouth gnawing on the purple loops of her intestines. It snarled at Temple. He thrust his bayonet into its eye and kicked it away.

Norris reached for him. He took her hand and knelt beside her.

"Benjamin wasn't your fault, Temple," she choked. "If I was a better soldier, I would have done it myself."

"You...you did good, Sergeant." The weight on his soul grew heavier with every word. "You taught us everything we needed to know."

She laughed weakly. "It's your Army, kid. I'm just in it."

He waited until her hand went limp before gently removing her gas mask and strapping it on. Sergeant Melissa Norris stared unseeing at the sky. Temple wiped the ashes from her face and closed her eyes.

***

Captain Andrada extended her extra-sensory perceptions into the madness of the noosphere. It was dangerous. Like an ocean disturbed by the coming of a tsunami, the eddies and currents of the Other

World threatened to sweep her away. She kept her astral-self close to her body while she searched for her quarry.

It wasn't a long search. Fiddler wasn't interested in hiding. It was closer to breaching than ever before. There was something else that caught Andrada's attention: a presence, following in Exalted Fiddler's wake. For a moment Andrada sensed a connection between it and the world of the living: an iron chain forged of guilt and regret.

"Major Lasky," she barked, closing her psychic eye. "Inform the general that we may see an increase in paranormal phenomenon in addition to Fiddler's presence."

"Yes, ma'am."

The commander's headset crackled.

"All Ironside elements, this is Rallypoint Tango. Be advised: enemy in the wire. I say again, enemy in the wire. Break. All artillery batteries are winchester on ammo. Requesting immediate suppression, danger close. How do you copy, over?"

There was a barely constrained terror in the speaker's voice. The din of battle and the screaming of clones in the background revealed how close the RTO was to the fighting.

It made her furious. Death was a perfectly acceptable fate for a soldier. Dying alone and forgotten was not.

"Rallypoint, this is Ironside Actual," the captain said. "Standby for immediate suppression. Keep your heads down and hang on. Old Ironsides is almost there." She switched to the *Behemoth's* interior channel. "Alright, Amir! I need you to whip this bitch until you're worried about blowing treads."

"Yes ma'am!"

Andrada settled into her seat and pulled the periscope to her eyes. She sighted in on the enemy position. She could see the fury of the battle and the host of aliens coming toward the human positions. Overhead drone imagery revealed another host of monsters behind the coral wall. The squids had committed only a third of their forces.

You're waiting for him, *aren't you?* She quickly plotted fire coordinates. *It makes no difference. I will devour your god and shit him out my exhaust pipes.*

"Alpha Gunner! Bravo Gunner!" she shouted.

"Gunner!" The soldiers assigned to *Behemoth's* twin 20-inch cannons responded from their stations below and behind her.

"Enemy troops in the open! High capacity, high explosive! Danger close! Confirm targets!"

"Targets identified!"

"Confirm danger close!"

"Confirmed!"

"Fire!" The word left her lips in a snarl, as though it alone could strike the enemy dead. "On the way!"

Both guns fired, making the *Behemoth* shudder on its treads. Andrada kept her eyes glued to the periscope.

"Target!" she shouted. The shells hit, hurling twin mushroom clouds of fire and ash into the sky. "Out-fucking-standing! Reload, and fire for effect!"

***

The sky split open and rained hell onto the enemy. The impact of the artillery rounds made Temple's teeth rattle. He lay prone, overwhelmed by the fury of the bombardment. The men around him screamed for mothers and gods that couldn't hear them as the world shook itself apart.

There is no place on this battlefield for men. We are caught in a war between gods and demons.

The impacting rounds finally shifted further out into the No Man's Land. Temple got to his feet. In a near stupor, he leaned back against the dirt wall of the trench. Cantu stalked toward him, the other infantryman's rage palpable even through his gas mask.

"Norris should've let you die." He gestured accusingly at their sergeant's bisected corpse. "She should've killed you, like you killed Benjamin."

"Yeah. She should have."

Cantu stopped. He stared at Temple, clenching and unclenching his fists.

The sudden coughing of an injured soldier lying next to Norris surprised both men out of the confrontation. Grievously wounded, the man rolled over onto his back.

"Please," he rasped. "Water."

Temple and Cantu helped him sit up.

"Here." Temple tried to attach Norris' canteen to the soldier's gas mask. "It's clean."

"Bastards tore me apart," the injured man rambled, lifting his arm. A deflated lung sagged between splintered ribs. "That's alright. I get the feeling I'll be back soon to return the favor."

He slumped forward.

"Easy," Cantu said, catching him. "Just drink the water."

"This guy knows." The wounded man pointed at Temple. "You've seen one of them. They're coming back to us, and they are fucking *pissed*."

The soldier's head lolled back. He seized for a few agonizing seconds before lying still. Temple shook as well. He tucked Norris' canteen away.

"What was he talking about?" Cantu asked, his voice returning to its usual mix of exhaustion and hostility.

"I don't know." Terror and guilt turned Temple's stomach into knots. "But I think I'm starting to lose it."

"Don't bitch out on me, Temple. We've come too far for you to run like Burley." He glanced up at the battlements. "We gotta get back up there. This artillery can't hold them at bay forever."

"Does it make any difference? We're finished either way."

"Yeah, but I'd rather die up there than stumbling around in a trench."

Ericks emerged from the disorganized mob of surviving infantrymen, the RTO covered in blood. None seemed to be his own.

"You see Burley?" Cantu asked.

"What was left of him." Ericks dropped his pack to the ground. He rummaged around for a moment before withdrawing a handful of magazines. "He didn't use any of his ammo." He tossed them to Cantu and Temple. They reloaded. "Shit. The squids got Sergeant Norris, too. Thought she'd be the one to survive this for sure."

"Can you get anyone on the radio?" Temple asked. The ashes were falling faster. It made him anxious. "Is this artillery coming from No. 3 Corps?"

"I can tell you right now that's No. 3 Corps," Ericks said, adjusting the radio's long whip antenna. "We don't have cannons anywhere near that powerful." He squeezed his hand mic. "Any station on this net, this is Crusader 1-2A. Radio check, over." Static answered him. "Any station, this is Crusader 1-2A, located at Echo Line. Be advised, we are black on ammo. Request guidance, over."

Temple heard a handful of garbled words behind the white noise.

"...back...enemy vector moving toward...-cho Line, be advis-..."

Ericks kicked his radio in frustration. "Piece of shit. Squid plasma bombardment must've fried it."

"It doesn't matter," Cantu said, pushing aside a dead clone blocking access to one of the ladders. "Come on. Let's die on our feet."

"God hates us too much to let us die," Ericks said.

I hope you're wrong, Temple thought as he climbed the ladder. The thought of living terrified him.

The alien attack had brutalized the battlements. Pillboxes burned up and down the line. Sandbag and concrete jersey barriers were toppled or pulled down. The concertina wire perimeter was hopelessly entangled with the corpses of clones and N'nogug.

The ferocious outgoing bombardment continued. The rounds landed closer to the far Northern reaches of the trench. Temple squinted through the falling ash and ruined mausoleums of the cemetery. A furious last stand played out at Alpha Line as a thousand clones hurled themselves through a curtain of fire to meet an unyielding wall of psycho-reactive steel.

The warning wail of sirens began. Temple took a knee behind a partially toppled sandbag wall. The cry of "Gas, gas, gas!" rose amid the shuffling of soldiers checking their masks in panic.

"Really?" Cantu yelled, at the enemy or the universe. "Can we catch a fucking break?!"

Temple's breath quickened. He tightened the straps of his own mask and offered a brief prayer to whatever god decided the manner of a soldier's death. His former ambivalence toward life suddenly seemed foolish.

I know I have to die today, but please...not like this.

The alien gas was invisible. The only sign of its arrival was when soldiers with bad seals or clogged canisters began screaming. Some tried to run. None made it far. A few put their pistols to their heads and blew their brains out before the alien miasma could do its worst.

It took the gas a moment to reach Ericks. He leaped up, shrieking. "Oh shit, oh shit, my mask!" He grappled with Temple in panic. "Help me! Please, god, it hurts!"

Temple pressed his hands to the side of Ericks' mask in a ridiculous and futile attempt to seal it. The RTO pulled away and stumbled backward. Ericks crawled to the edge of the trench. He pulled off his gas mask and took in a gasping breath before vomiting. A vicious seizure wracked his body.

Temple forced himself to watch Ericks drowning in his own blood. *This death is yours, too. Another one you couldn't save. Another to avenge.*

Something massive rose from behind the Voidborn coral perimeter as the miasma savaged the trench system. It surged through a rip in time and space, a portal to frozen realms illuminated by the hateful light of zombie stars.

Dead soldiers whispered in Temple's ear. *Ubolzhach is coming. Ubolzhach is here.*

"What the fuck is that?" Cantu whispered.

Blood and ashes fell from the sky, and a demon god emerged from the warp gate. It pulled itself into reality, its crustacean talons digging into the earth. Three pairs of crushing claws, big enough to snap an Abrams tank in two, clacked noisily. Massive particle beam cannons had been crudely sutured onto its scaly hide. Skinned, fleshless human bodies were impaled on the huge spikes covering its shell.

It opened its mouth and roared. Acidic drool splattered from its maw, sizzling on the sacred earth of Arlington. The particle weapons on its shoulders leveled toward Alpha Section to the North and fired. Temple covered his eyes with his hands, the brightness of the weapon's discharge nearly blinding him. A mushroom cloud blossomed across the trench line. Alpha Section was reduced to a crater, destroyed by the terrible power of the alien god.

Hundreds of true Voidborn followed in Ubolzhach's wake. The makers and masters of the clones and the N'nogug were far larger than the rabid beasts they used as cannon fodder. Their calcareous shells were as hard as titanium. Each of their dozen barbed tentacles clutched arcane devices, as much instruments of torture as they were weapons. Unlike the clones, they could speak, but the alien words made Temple wish he was deaf. They raised their scale-covered tentacles in gestures of supplication and worship to their dreadful deity.

The Voidborn opened fire. Temple flattened himself against the ground. Cantu spoke the words of the Infantryman's Creed as though they were an incantation against evil.

"Always I press on." His voice cracked and shook. "Through the foe. To the objective. To triumph over all. If necessary, I will fight to my death."

The scattered return fire coming from Echo Line was quickly obliterated by precise particle weapon fire. The Voidborn scuttled across the battlefield. Small arms fire bounced off their shells, their hideous shrieks sounding like laughter.

It took everything in Temple's power to raise his rifle. He aimed through the clouds of swirling dust, all that was left of the world he loved, and pulled the trigger.

The explosion that struck the advancing Voidborn was strong enough to send a wall of ash and debris rushing over them. Temple furiously wiped his lenses clear. The ground trembled. The air ignited in serpentine trails from the fury of the outgoing rounds.

A god of titanium and fire rolled over the ruins of Echo Line, its massive treads carrying it over the trench. The super-tank parked at the very edge of the hill, two hundred meters from where Temple lay prone. Thick plumes of smoke curled from its two menacing main guns. The words *Behold, the Behemoth!* were painted above a cartoon of a ferocious whale devouring a kraken. A harpoon gun the size of a pickup truck sat just before the tank's uppermost cupola.

The *Behemoth* sounded a challenge through war-horns mounted on its armored prow. The rage of an arriving army answered it. The armored might of the No. 3 Corps rolled into position across the trenches. Tracked M2A3 Bradley Fighting Vehicles and eight-wheeled Stryker assault craft dropped ramp, disgorging a thousand shouting infantrymen. M1 Abrams battle tanks set up staggered positions and began immediate suppressive fires on the enemy with 120mm cannons.

"I don't believe it," Cantu said. "Burley was actually right for once."

The hatch on the *Behemoth*'s command cupula opened. A lone figure leaned out, gripping the handles of a massive harpoon gun.

The blade of the weapon glowed white from the power of its psycho-reactive runes. She shouted something, her voice lost on the hot wind generated by countless high explosives.

The horns sounded again: this time, the familiar bugle notes that signaled the charge. Dozens of 25mm chain-guns and 120mm cannons mounted on the Behemoth's sponsons opened fire as it rolled toward the enemy. Its smaller kin swiftly got on line, forming an invincible iron wall that the infantry used as mobile cover.

No. 3 Corps infantrymen clambered up the battlements around the survivors of Echo Line, running to back up their armor support. Only one stopped: a trooper with a near-fatal head wound, who glanced briefly at Temple before following after the No. 3 Corp line-breakers.

Temple leaped to his feet to follow. Cantu grabbed his arm.

"You've got three mags left. This is No. 3 Corps' fight, you're gonna get yourself killed!"

"I don't care." Temple fought to free himself. "I have to do this!"

"Why, goddammit?!"

"Because of Benjamin." Saying it aloud did nothing to ease his guilt. "It's the only way to set things right."

"That's bullshit!" For the first time in weeks, Cantu looked him in the eye. "You saved him, Temple. You spared him when none of us could."

"I asked him to switch places with me. It should have been *me* burning in the truck. Not him."

Cantu let go of his arm. Temple turned without hesitation. He heard Cantu shouting after him as he lowered his bayonet and charged.

***

Andrada didn't climb down from the cupola despite Major Lasky's insistence. Her adjutant didn't understand. She needed to witness the sky splitting apart, to hear the blood-soaked ash cyclones shrieking as they kissed the earth, to feel the fury of war while she directed her brigade, to suck in the taste of death with every breath.

"Tertiary guns, focus fire on the Voidborn dismounts!" she snapped through her headset. "All secondary weapons, direct fire to support 14th Regiment's advance from the west! 120s, direct lay on the enemy perimeter! Crack the reef open!"

Heavy particle cannon fire slammed into the *Behemoth*. Warning sirens and the screams of the wounded rose from below her. She ignored them.

Let the Behemoth *burn. So long as She crushes their damned, heathen god beneath her treads first.*

The *Behemoth* formed the tip of an iron spear, rushing toward the Voidborn defenses. The writhing polyps that created the organic wall erupted in clouds of inky liquid. Some of the Voidborn tried attacking the tank as it smashed through their line. Heavy flamethrower ports reduced them to clumps of putrid jelly.

Andrada took no pleasure in their deaths. Gods cared nothing for the deaths of mortals. There was only one enemy, one kill, that mattered.

Reality itself trembled at the sound of Ubolzhach's voice. The demon's thousand eyes stared balefully at the *Behemoth,* as though sizing up its new adversary.

"Target!" Andrada shouted. "1,000 meters westward! Enemy HVT in the open! High capacity, high explosive! All guns, direct lay! Amir, bring us 30 degrees westward and step on it!"

A chorus of affirmations came over her headset. The turret rotated. Andrada gripped the harpoon controls through hands soaked in blood. The *Behemoth* changed course enough to ensure a devastating broadside of the main and secondary weapons.

Ubolzhach came at them. Its particle beams glistened, the deity trampling its worshippers underfoot to get to them.

The *Behemoth* and Ubolzhach fired on one another. The alien's particle cannons sheared one of the main guns in half. Stars burst before Andrada's eyes. Her ears bled from the sound of the blast-wave. She shook her head, desperate to right herself.

"We've taken major tread damage," Amir grunted over her headset, struggling to keep control. "There are fires on decks 1 and 2. Fire suppression systems aren't activating. We've lost turret rotation for the main guns."

"Bring us about, then!" Andrada braced herself against the hatch. "Point us right at the bastard and give me a clean shot!"

The alien god circled. Amir turned the *Behemoth*. Ubolzhach shrieked in the hateful language of the Voidborn, singing praises to deities even more loathsome than it. It snapped its huge claws together in a challenge, despite bleeding from a hundred wounds.

Ubolzhach charged. Andrada cursed. "Come on, Amir!" she aimed the harpoon, knowing it was out of range. "Get her 'round, damn it!"

Smoke rose from the cabin below her. Andrada ignored the heat of the flames and the screams of the wounded crew members. There was just the monster before her, and the murderous rage that propelled her onward.

Amir forced the super-tank to turn about. The crosshairs on the harpoon lined up. Andrada fired. The massive projectile punched into Ubolzhach just beneath its shell. The 24-inch cable anchoring it to the *Behemoth* tightened immediately. Andrada tilted back her head and howled with the lightning.

"From hell's heart, you son of a bitch! From hell's fucking heart!"

Ubolzhach tried to pull away. The runes on the harpoon's blade shone brilliantly even beneath its flesh. "All ahead full!" Andrada shouted. "All guns, fire at will!"

The *Behemoth* blasted its shell to pieces. The gigantic demon roared. Two of its crusher arms disappeared, reduced to stumps spewing acidic pus. It stumbled, steam rising where chunks of its flesh had been vaporized.

Ubolzhach locked eyes with Andrada. It fired again. The heat from the blast made the skin on her neck and hands blister. The particle beam carved through the very center of the *Behemoth*. Andrada felt its engines die, even as its unstoppable momentum carried it forward.

Ubolzhach waited to embrace them. Andrada snarled a curse. The demon filled her field of vision as its remaining claws grasped the *Behemoth*. It savaged the tank with its barbed tentacles, even as the weight of the vast war machine shattered its lower limbs and carapace.

Andrada came eye to eye with the demon before it managed to flip the *Behemoth*. She spat her defiance, reveling in the terrible wounds she had inflicted as she was flung free from the cupola.

***

The wreck of the *Behemoth* loomed from the swirling ash blizzard. The war machine lay on its side, consumed in flames. Superheated radioactive material burned its way through the fallen god's thick, armored skin.

Temple thought of Benjamin, trapped in the burning Humvee, and the bullet to the back of his skull that had finally released his brother from such torment.

He approached the wreck with only his yatagan bayonet. He wasn't sure what had happened to his rifle or gas mask. Every breath made his lungs ache.

The tank commander lay on the ground, legs twisted at an odd angle. She was alive, barely, her gaze fixed on the god in fire-lit shadows.

Ubolzhach continued its rampage. It was wounded, maybe gravely so, but its guns kept the tank assault at bay. Voidborn reinforcements rushed to counter-charge from their shattered defensive walls. It was only a matter of time before some headed his way.

And then this nightmare will finally end.

The officer squinted at Temple, then looked past him at something he could not see. She laughed at some joke only she could hear.

"You've brought ghosts with you, soldier," she said. "And they're killing you."

"I just want this to end."

"Don't we all?"

Ubolzhach stopped its rampage. It turned, slowly, as though sensing Temple's presence. Its stalk eyes twisted and writhed until at last its hateful gaze settled upon him.

The injured colonel drew a pistol and fired. The 9mm rounds bounced off Ubolzhach's armored carapace.

"For hate's sake," she said. "I spit at thee."

Her words trailed off. Her arm fell limp at her side. Even in death, she did not look away.

Ubolzhach roared. The ground shook at its approach. The dreadful praise of the Voidborn reached a fever pitch. Its guns fired at distant targets even as it continued toward him.

Temple raised his blade to meet it. He laughed at the insanity of it; one man, little more than a boy, marching out to defy a god.

He raised the saber high. Ubolzhach's shadow fell over him. The light of the runes glowed bright enough to cast strange shadows across the battlefield. White and red flames dripped off the blade until the entire saber was consumed.

Benjamin cried out from beside him. The ghost appeared from the swirling mists, speaking words in a language known only to the dead. He was answered from across the battlefield in a haunting chorus that silenced the ceaseless worship of the enemy.

Reality split at the edge of the saber. A host of spectral warriors materialized, wreathed in hellfire and screaming with voices as old as the nation that had buried them.

The ghosts of Arlington tore into the Voidborn army. They tore aliens limb from limb, and hurled bolts of eldritch lightning. Four hundred thousand souls, disturbed from their sacred rest, flowed through Temple's connection to his dead brother, and found new purpose where his saber tore reality apart.

Temple charged, screaming. The ghosts took hold of him, lifting him toward the devil god, hurling him headlong into oblivion. He heard the soul of Andrada, the tank commander, and felt her burning hands grip the bayonet with him as they drove it into the Voidborn god.

Ubolzhach splintered. Light poured from fissures that cracked the demon into a thousand pieces, radiating out from the wounds the *Behemoth* had inflicted. Its toxic innards turned to molten gold as the bisected pieces of its corpse fell to the earth.

The Voidborn broke when their god died. The armored advance overran their positions and destroyed their artillery. Every soldier still able to fight abandoned the trenches and charged to clear the battlefield of any remaining hostiles.

Temple rose from the wreckage of the demon's corpse to see Benjamin watching him. The ghost's expression was blank, devoid of pity or hate, forgiveness or remorse.

"It's my fault you died," Temple said.

He sank to his knees. His bayonet had dissolved into ashes, leaving behind a jagged shard of steel. Temple closed his eyes and held it to his throat.

It was Cantu that saved him: Cantu, who had crossed the battlefield after him, who threw down his rifle and took Temple in his arms.

"It wasn't your fault. Goddamit. It wasn't your fault." He spoke, and Benjamin's ghost mouthed the words in silent echoes. "You have to let it go."

The ashes fell. Temple released the bayonet and wept. With that, Cantu unscrewed the cap from Norris' canteen and washed the filth from Temple's face.

END

CONTRIBUTOR LIST

Chris McInally, editor

Born in Glasgow, Scotland, Chris now lives in Australia with his wife and son. In addition to holding an Honours Degree in environmental history he has a Ph.D in Irish history. His Ph.D dissertation was the basis for his first non-fiction book, *FROM BLOODY SUNDAY TO BOBBY SANDS*, published by the James Connolly Association Australia in 2020.

A former ISKA no. 2 ranked competitor for the state of Victoria, Chris continues to train in various martial arts.

An avid reader as a child it was perhaps inevitable that he would one day turn to writing himself. His favourite authors include George R.R. Martin, Steve Alten, Matthew Reilly, R.L. Stine, James Herbert, Greig Beck, Joe Abercrombie and Jeremy Robinson (among others).

Since 2016 he had published five fiction titles: *APEX* and its sequel, along with the standalone novels, *FLUX, DEEP BLACK,* and *THE VALLEY OF TOOTH & CLAW*. All of which are available through independent publisher Severed Press.

His forthcoming novel, *RELICT,* is scheduled to be released through Screaming Banshee Press in mid/late 2021.

Join Chris on Twitter @chrismcinally5

Facebook: https://www.facebook.com/AuthorChrisMcInally.

Dan Rabarts, writer

Story: 'Softbait'

Dan Rabarts is an award-winning author and editor, four-time recipient of New Zealand's Sir Julius Vogel Award and three-time winner of the Australian Shadows Award, occasional sailor of sailing things, part-time metalhead and father of two wee miracles in a house on a hill under the southern sun. Together with Lee Murray, he co-writes the *Path of Ra* crime-noir thriller series from Raw Dog Screaming Press (*Hounds of the Underworld, Teeth of the Wolf, Blood of the Sun*) and co-edited the flash-fiction horror anthology *Baby Teeth - Bite-sized Tales of Terror*, and *At The Edge*, an anthology of Antipodean dark fiction. His steampunk-grimdark-comic fantasy series *Children of Bane* starts with *Brothers of the Knife* and continues in *Sons of the Curse* and *Sisters of Spindrift* (Omnium Gatherum Media). Dan's science fiction, dark fantasy and horror short stories have been published in numerous venues worldwide. He also regularly narrates and produces for podcasts and audiobooks. Find him at dan.rabarts.com.

Daniele Bonfanti, writer

Story: 'The Shattering'

Daniele Bonfanti is an Italian speculative fiction and adventure writer, as well as an active member of the Horror Writers Association and a Splatterpunk Award nominee.

His English credits include stories in the Stoker-nominated anthologies *THE BEAUTY OF DEATH*, 1 & 2 (Independent Legions, 2016-2017), and in the deluxe hardcover *SUPERNATURAL HORROR* (Flame Tree, 2017). His novella *GAME* received a shortlist

Honourable Mention in Datlow's *THE BEST HORROR OF THE YEAR, VOL. 9*, and another story was on the longlist the following year. Bonfanti co-edited the anthology *MONSTERS OF ANY KIND* with Alessandro Manzetti. He has also translated books from Italian and Spanish into English, for imprints such as Independent Legions, Omnium Gatherum and Necro Publishing; authors include Manzetti, Paolo Di Orazio, Santiago Eximeno, and Stefano Cardoselli, with whom he also created the graphic novel *UNSTOPPABLE*. Bonfanti already appeared in Screaming Banshee's *ABERRATIONS*.

His Italian credits include the novels *MELODIA* and *QUINTESSENZA*, several short stories, three co-edited anthologies, and scores of non-fiction articles for the popular print magazine, *HERA*. He has translated into Italian novels by Clive Barker, Ramsey Campbell, Brian Keene, Skipp & Spector, Richard Laymon; as well as long and short fiction by Joe R. Lansdale, Harlan Ellison, Peter Straub, Poppy Z. Brite, John A. Lindqvist, Jack Ketchum, and Stephen King.

Bonfanti lives on Lake Como, Italy, with his wife and daughters. Outside of work, he is a mountaineer, open-water swimmer, trail runner, kayaker and traveller, enjoying adventure as well as writing about it.

You can visit his website: www.danielebonfanti.com

William Meikle, writer

Story: 'Labyrinth'

William is a Scottish writer, now living in Canada, with over thirty novels published in the genre press and more than 300 short story credits in thirteen countries. He has books available from a variety of publishers including Dark Regions Press and Severed Press and his work has appeared in a large number of professional anthologies and magazines. He lives in Newfoundland with whales, bald eagles and icebergs for company. When he's not writing he drinks beer, plays guitar, and dreams of fortune and glory.

Lucas Pederson, writer

Story: 'Bonesaw Ridge'

Lucas Pederson is an American novelist and short story writer of horror, dark fantasy, young adult and science fiction. He lives in a small Iowa town with his family and they're all pretty sure their cat is an alien.

Alister Hodge, writer

Story: 'A Man of His Word'

Alister is a Sydney based author, writing within the genres of horror, thriller and fantasy. During the last three years, he has published five novels through Severed Press, Luzifer Verlag and Tantor Media. The German translation of his most recent release, a creature feature titled *The Cavern*, is an Amazon international bestseller, having sat at the top of its category for over four months. Outside of fiction writing, Alister works as a Nurse Practitioner in a busy metropolitan Emergency Department and has also authored numerous journal and textbook publications.

Fiction Publications:

Hodge A (2018) *Plague War: Outbreak*. Severed Press.

Hodge A (2018) *Plague War 2: Pandemic*. Severed Press.

Hodge A. (2018) *Plague War 3: Retaliation*. Severed Press.

Hodge A (2019) *The Cavern*. Severed Press

Hodge A (2020) 'True Mettle' in *Blood, Brains & Bullets*. Screaming Banshee Press

Hodge A (2020) *The Cavern: Das Grauen aus der Tiefe*. Luzifer Verlag

Hodge A. (2020) *Escape from Viperob Island*. Severed Press

Hodge A (2020) 'The Three Brothers' in *Aberrations*. Screaming Banshee Press

Hodge A (To be released 2021) *Empire of Blood and Sand*. Screaming Banshee Press

----

R.F. Blackstone, writer

Story: 'Black Ice'

R.F. Blackstone has been writing for over 15 years, starting in the hallowed world of scripting. After many would-be deals with the Devil, R.F. said "Screw it!", then picked up the mantle of novelist and has never looked back. His published works include, *Big Smoke* and *Kaiju World* (both released through Severed Press) as well as *Flicker* and *The Book of Spite*.

Lee Murray, writer

Story: 'Into the Geyserland'

Lee Murray is a multi-award-winning author-editor from Aotearoa-New Zealand (Sir Julius Vogel, Australian Shadows), and a three-time Bram Stoker Award®-nominee. Her work includes military thrillers, the Taine McKenna Adventures, supernatural crime-noir series The Path of Ra (with Dan Rabarts), and debut collection *Grotesque: Monster Stories*. Her latest anthology projects are *Black Cranes: Tales of Unquiet Women*, co-edited with Geneve Flynn, and Midnight Echo #15. She is co-founder of Young NZ Writers and of the Wright-Murray Residency for Speculative Fiction Writers, HWA Mentor of the Year for 2019, NZSA Honorary Literary Fellow, and Grimshaw Sargeson Fellow for 2021. Read more at leemurray.info.

Website: https://www.leemurray.info/

Facebook: https://www.facebook.com/groups/MonsterReaders

Twitter: https://twitter.com/leemurraywriter

Instagram: https://www.instagram.com/leemurray2656/

Bookbub: https://www.bookbub.com/authors/lee-murray

Amazon: https://www.amazon.com/Lee-Murray/e/B0068FHSC4

Dustin Dreyling, writer

Story: 'The Bubble Bursts'

Dustin Dreyling is a lifelong native of Saint Paul, Minnesota. A fan of almost all things sci-fi and horror, he lives there with the love of his life, Melissa, and their fur and scale babies. A devout fan of authors like Jeremy Robinson, Jeff Strand, Brian Keene, and Tim Curran; their works have been a large influence on him. These are in addition to horror greats like H.P. Lovecraft and Stephen King. So far, Dreyling has had stories in anthologies published by Wild Hunt Press, including *The Experiment,* volume one of *Duel of the Monsters,* and volume two of *Attack of the Kaiju: The Next Wave.* His premiere novel, *Primordial Soup: The First Batch*, was also published by Wild Hunt Press at the end of 2020.

Justin Coates, writer

Story: 'The Apocalypse Drive'

Justin Coates writes out of Livonia, Michigan, where he lives with his wife and two sons. His military science fiction has been published in a variety of anthologies, including those associated with the hit Netflix series *Love, Death and Robots*. Follow him on Facebook (facebook. com/justinacoates) and Twitter (twitter.com/dreary_terrors)

Printed in Great Britain
by Amazon

36963879R00119